A TIME TO LAUGH

Funny Stories for Children

Also edited by Sara and Stephen Corrin

STORIES FOR UNDER-FIVES

MORE STORIES FOR UNDER-FIVES

STORIES FOR SIX-YEAR-OLDS

STORIES FOR SEVEN-YEAR-OLDS

MORE STORIES FOR SEVEN-YEAR-OLDS

STORIES FOR EIGHT-YEAR-OLDS

STORIES FOR NINE-YEAR-OLDS

STORIES FOR TEN-YEAR-OLDS

IMAGINE THAT! FIFTEEN FANTASTIC TALES

PET STORIES FOR CHILDREN

THE FABER BOOK OF CHRISTMAS STORIES

ROUND THE CHRISTMAS TREE

ONCE UPON A RHYME: 101 POEMS FOR YOUNG CHILDREN

THE FABER BOOK OF MODERN FAIRY TALES

THE FABER BOOK OF FAVOURITE FAIRY TALES

A TIME TO LAUGH
Funny Stories for Children

edited by
Sara and Stephen Corrin

illustrated by
Gerald Rose

faber and faber
LONDON · BOSTON

A Time to Laugh: Thirty Stories for Young Children
first published in 1972
by Faber and Faber Limited
3 Queen Square London WC1N 3AU
Reprinted in 1975
This selection of stories
first published in 1989
Reprinted 1990

Printed in England by Clays Ltd, St Ives plc

This selection © Faber and Faber Limited, 1989
Illustrations © Faber and Faber Limited, 1972, 1989

British Library Cataloguing in Publication Data is available

ISBN 0–571–13416–5

Contents

Acknowledgements

We are most grateful to the following publishers, authors and agents for permission to include these stories:

Abelard-Schuman for 'The Emperor's Oblong Pancake' by Peter Hughes.

Evans Brothers (Books) Limited for 'The Wishing-skin' from *Ten Minute Tales* by Rhoda Power.

Blackie and Son Limited for 'Clever Oonagh' from *Fairy Tales from the British Isles* by Amabel Williams-Ellis.

Hutchinson Publishing Group Limited for 'Mrs Pepperpot Buys Macaroni' from *Little Old Mrs Pepperpot* by Alf Proysen.

William Heinemann Limited for 'The Ju-ju Man' from *Cherry Stones* by Ruth Ainsworth.

The Estate of A. A. Milne and Curtis Brown Limited for 'Eeyore Loses a Tail and Pooh Finds One' from *Winnie the Pooh* by A. A. Milne.

Blackie and Son Limited for 'The Chatterbox' by Amabel Williams-Ellis and Moura Budberg.

We should like to thank Mrs S. Stonebridge,

Principal Children's Librarian, Royal Borough of Kensington and Chelsea, Mrs Mary Clunes, Children's Librarian, Golders Green Public Library, Hazel Wilkinson, Mary Junor, Schools Librarian, Barnet, and Eileen Leach, Children's Librarian, Watford Library; for their ever-willing and invaluable help and advice; and, of course, Phyllis Hunt of Faber and Faber for constant guidance and encouragement.

A Note for the Story-teller

What do children laugh at? Although as adults we tend to think that their sense of humour is cruder and simpler than ours, closer analysis suggests that the basic stuff of humour is the same for child and man alike: the little man outwitting the braggart and bully; the supercilious and haughty brought to justice; the theme of 'the smile on the face of the tiger'; slapstick; sweet revenge, as in 'The Fox and the Stork'; ingratitude punished by elegant cunning, as in 'The Tiger, the Brahmin and the Jackal'.

The nagging wife theme, recurrent in folktale, where the woman receives her just desserts, is sometimes counterbalanced in other tales when the wife becomes the heroine, her cunning and wit helping her husband out of a scrape. In 'Mrs Pepperpot Buys Macaroni' is an additional source of humour: the diminutive Mrs Pepperpot mistaken for a mouse by the embarrassed shopkeeper who adopts comic means to cover up his discomfiture.

The appeal to the child's rough sense of justice finds a never-failing response. The preposterous

11

antics of Little Claus, robbed by his powerful neighbour of his only means of livelihood, are accepted in
spite of their outrageous improbability. The brave
little tailor illustrates the dream of the weak becoming
stout-hearted and reflects, perhaps, the fantasies of
the child in his play when he sees himself as the
King of the Castle.

Such is the stuff these tales are made of and such
is the stuff that has made them survive.

Clever Oonagh

There was once a giant in Ireland called Cucullin, and another giant that was also supposed to be a mighty warrior, though he wasn't near so big. His name was Fin.

There's many a terrible tale told about these two – Cucullin and Fin – and their great and famous deeds and their battles. But there's one story about them and about Fin's wife, Oonagh, which is different. Maybe it's just a tale that was told round about the country by those who were sick and tired of hearing only about their killing and slaughtering and the great deeds. Perhaps a few people wanted to have the laugh of them.

Now Fin had his house at the very top of a steep hill called Knockmany, which wasn't really just such a very convenient place for a house, because, you see, whichever way the wind blew, it always blew up there. Another thing was that, when her husband Fin was away, Oonagh had always to go down to the very bottom of the steep hill to the spring before she could draw a drop of water, and then she had

13

to carry her full pails all the way to the top again.

But all the same 'twas a good spot for a house in one way, for being perched up like that at the very top of Knockmany Hill, Fin could see all ways – North, South, East and West – and that gave him a good warning if any of his enemies should take it into their heads to pay him a visit. Fin wasn't one to like being taken by surprise. He had yet another way of getting a warning, as well as keeping a good look-out. He would put his thumb into his mouth till it touched one special tooth, right at the back, and then the thumb would tell him what was coming to pass.

Well, one day, when all seemed peaceful, Fin was sitting with his wife, Oonagh, when she saw that he had put his thumb in his mouth.

'What are you doing that for, Fin?' says she.

'Oh, my grief and sorrow, he's coming!' said Fin as soon as he had pulled out his thumb and could speak plain, and she saw that he looked as miserable as a wet Sunday.

'Who's coming?' asked Oonagh.

'That horrid beast of an old Cucullin, no less,' answered Fin.

Now, as Oonagh well knew, though Fin was near as tall and big as a round-tower, Cucullin was bigger still and was an enemy that Fin didn't want to meet, no, not for all the world. All the giants for miles around were afraid of Cucullin. When he was angry and gave a stamp with his foot, the whole country shook. Once, by a blow of his fist, he had flattened

14

a thunderbolt till it was flat as a pancake, and ever after he kept it in his pocket to show to anyone who offered to fight with him. Fin was a match for most of the rest of the giants, and had even boasted that the great Cucullin had never – so far – come near him for fear he would get a drubbing. But now, oh grief and sorrow! Cucullin, no less, was on his way, and Fin didn't like the idea – no, not at all!

'How to get round such a terrible fellow, or what to do, I don't know,' went on Fin to his wife in a very doleful tone. 'If I run away while there's still time I shall be a laughing-stock to all the other giants, and a terrible disgrace will be on me. But how to fight with a giant that makes a pancake out of a thunderbolt with one blow of his fist, and that shakes the whole country with one stamp of his foot, I don't know!'

'How far has he got?' asks Oonagh.

'As far as Dungannon,' answers Fin.

'How soon will he be here?' asks she.

'Tomorrow about two o'clock,' answers he, and then he adds with a groan, 'And meet him I shall for my thumb tells me so.'

'Now, now, my dear! Don't fret and don't be cast down!' answers Oonagh. 'Let's see if I can't be the one to bring you out of your great trouble!'

'For the love of all the saints, Oonagh my darling, do what you can! Else for sure I'll either be skinned like a rabbit before your eyes, or else have my name disgraced before the whole tribe of giants. Oh, my

15

grief! Oh, my sorrow! If this isn't just a regular earth-quake of a fellow, and him with a pancake in his pocket that was once a thunderbolt!'

'For shame on you, Fin! Be easy now! Pancake, did you say? See now if I can't treat that bully boy to some feeding that'll give him a sore tooth! Leave your moaning and lamenting now, Fin! If I can't get around and circumvent that great lump of a fellow, never trust Oonagh again.'

With that she went to where her skeins of wool were hung out to dry after she had dyed them and she took nine long strands of all the colours she had. She plaited the wool-threads three and three, and when it was done she tied one plait round her right arm, one round her right ankle and the third and longest she tied right round her, over her heart.

She'd done all this several times before, when Fin was in trouble, so his mind got a bit firmer when he saw what she was at, for the truth is she hadn't ever failed yet when she had got the threads on her.

'Is there time for me to go round to the neigh-bours?' Oonagh asked.

'There is time,' said Fin. So off she set and she went to this one and that. When she came back Fin saw that she had borrowed a whole load of griddles – which are thin irons, like huge plates, for making scones or flat bread over a turf fire. Then he saw how she kneaded enough dough to make as many griddle loaves as she had irons. One she cooked in the proper way and made a good round flat loaf of it – as big as a cart-wheel nearly – but all the rest were made in a very strange way, for she made them two-sided, each with an iron griddle hidden in the middle. As each one was done, she put it away in the bread-cupboard. Then she made a big milk cheese and she boiled a whole side of bacon, set it to cool, and began to boil a sackful of cabbages.

By this time it was evening, the evening of the day before Cucullin was to come, and the last thing Oonagh did was to light a high smoking bonfire on the hill outside and to put her fingers in her mouth to give three whistles. This was to let Cucullin know that strangers were invited to Knockmany, for that was the way that the Irish, long ago, would be giving a sign to travellers that they could come in. Oonagh didn't tell Fin about her plans that night, but she did ask him a few things about Cucullin, and one of the things that Fin told her was that Cucullin's mighty strength lay in just the one place, and that was the middle finger of his right hand.

Next morning, as you can guess, Fin was on the look-out, and after a while he saw how his enemy Cucullin – as tall as a church tower – was striding along across the valley.

Back into the house went Fin and his face was as white as Oonagh's milk cheese when he was telling her the news. But Oonagh only smiled, she had something ready for Fin too.

'Now, Fin dear! Take it more easy! Be guided by me. Here's the cradle that the children are too old for now, and here's a white bonnet, and here's a nightgown of mine that will look for all the world like a baby's robe when you have it on over your shirt. Dress yourself up, lie down snug in the cradle, and cover yourself with the quilt, say nothing, and be guided by me, for this day you must pass for your own child.'

Fin was shaking with fear and he was scarcely tucked up, when there came a regular thunder of a knock on the door.

'Come in and welcome!' cried Oonagh, and, with that, a great huge man twice as big as old Fin, opened the door. And who was it but the mighty Cucullin himself, as punctual to his time as the stars themselves.

'God save all here,' says he in a great rumbling voice. 'And is this where the famous Fin lives?'

'Indeed and it is! Come in and rest, honest man.'

'It's Mrs Fin you'll be?' says he, coming in and sitting down.

'Indeed and I am, and a fine strong husband I have,' says she.

'Aye,' says he, 'he has the name of being one of the best giants in Ireland, but all the same there's one come that is very willing to try to get the better of him in a fair fight.'

'Dear me!' says Oonagh. 'Isn't that a grievous pity now, for he left the house in a fury this very morning at the first light. Word had come that a great big bully of a giant by the name of Cucullin had gone

18

down to look for him on the northern coast of the sea – the place where the Irish giants are building their causeway to get to Scotland. Saints above! But I hope for the poor ignorant fellow's sake that he doesn't find Fin, for Fin'll make paste of Cucullin this day, he's in such a fury!'

'It's I am Cucullin, and it's I that am after fighting with Fin!' answered Cucullin, frowning. 'This twelve-month I'm after looking for him, and it's Fin that will be ground to paste, not me!'

'My sorrow! I'm thinking that you never saw Fin,' said Oonagh, shaking her head.

'How could I see Fin,' answered Cucullin, 'and him dodging all the while to get away from me like as if he was a snipe on a bog?'

'Fin dodging to get away from you, is it, you poor little creature?' says Oonagh. 'I tell you it'll be the black day for you if ever you do see Fin, and let's only hope the wild furious temper that is on him now will have cooled a bit, or else it's rushing to your death you'd be. Rest here a while and when you go it's me that will pray to the holy saints that you never catch up with Fin.'

Cucullin began to wonder a bit about such words, so he didn't speak for a while, and presently Oonagh said, looking about her:

'Isn't that just a terrible wind that's blowing in at the door and making the smoke come down! Fin always helps me when it does that. As he's from home, perhaps you'd be civil enough to do the job

19

for me?'

'What job is that?' asked Cucullin.

'Oh, just to turn the house round for me. That's what Fin always does.'

This made Cucullin wonder a bit more. However, he got up and then Oonagh noticed that as he stood there he pulled at the middle finger of his right hand till it gave three little cracks, and she remembered how Fin had told her that it was in this finger that Cucullin's mighty strength lay.

Well, after that he stumped outside on his great legs, put his two great arms round the house and turned it round, just as Oonagh had asked him to do.

Fin, hiding in the cradle, felt ready to die with fear to see the like of that, for of course he never had turned the house for Oonagh, no, not in all the long time they'd been married.

But Oonagh, who was outside with Cucullin, gave a sweet smile and a plain 'thank you', making out that turning a whole house round was as easy as opening a door.

'Since you're so civil, perhaps you'd do another obliging thing for me, Fin being away,' says she.

'What obliging thing is that?' asked Cucullin.

'Nothing very great,' says she. 'But after this spell of dry weather we've been after enduring, I'm having to go down the hill for every drop of water. Only last night Fin promised me he'd get at a spring of water there is under the rocks at the back. But he left home in such a temper, chasing after you to fight you, that he forgot all about it. I'll have a bite of dinner ready for you, if you'll just pull the rocks asunder for me.'

So she brought Cucullin down to see the place, and indeed it was all rock and part of the mountain itself, with only one small crack in it, so that you could scarcely hear the water gurgling underneath.

It was plain from the look on Cucullin's face that he didn't like the job. However, he pulled his finger three times and took another look, then he pulled it three times again, and had another look, and still he didn't like what he saw, for the job was no less than to rend the mountain itself.

However, after he had pulled his finger yet three times more – that was nine times in all – he stepped down. This time he tore a great cleft in the side of the mountain, and it was four hundred feet deep and half a mile long. (It's there to this day – Lumford's Glen they call it.)

'That's very obliging of you I'm sure,' says Oonagh. 'And now away back to the house, for you to get a bite of dinner, for Fin would be blaming me if I let you go without, even if you are enemies, and even if it's only our own humble fare that I can set before you.'

Fin, you remember, was still in the cradle, and hadn't seen what had been going on outside, but all the same he was quaking and shivering to see Cucullin coming back with Oonagh and sitting down

21

at the table.

Oonagh served the giant with two big cans of butter, the whole side of bacon, and she had the whole sack of cabbages ready boiled for him. Last of all she brought out a pile of the big round flat loaves that she had baked the day before.

'Help yourself, and welcome,' says she.

So Cucullin started on the bacon and cabbages and then he picked up one of the big flat loaves and opened his mouth wide to take a huge bite out of it. But he had scarcely bitten into that bread before he let out a terrible yell.

'Blood and fury!' cries he.

'What's the matter?' asks Oonagh.

'Matter enough!' cries he. 'Here's two of my best teeth cracked. What kind of bread is this?'

'Why,' said Oonagh, making out that she was very much surprised, 'that's only Fin's bread! Even his child in the cradle there can eat it!' With that she took the one flat loaf that hadn't got a griddle inside it, and she went across to Fin where he lay in the cradle, and gave him the bread and a hard nudge.

Cucullin watched, and sure enough the thing in the cradle took a huge bite out of the bread and then started munching.

'Here's another loaf for you, Cucullin!' says Oonagh, shaking her head as if she pitied him. 'Maybe this one'll be softer for you.'

But this one had a griddle inside it as well, and when he tried to bite it Cucullin let out a yell that

22

was louder than the first, for he'd bitten harder, not liking the way Oonagh had seemed to pity him.

This yell of Cucullin's was so loud that it frightened Fin into letting out a yell as well.

'There now, you've gone and upset the child!' says Oonagh. 'If you're not able to eat Fin's bread, why can't you say so quietly?'

But Cucullin hadn't got an answer to that, for he was beginning to feel a bit frightened. What with turning the house, and what with tearing up the mountain, and now what with seeing Fin's child, though it was still in its cradle, munching that terrible bread before his very eyes, he was beginning to think that it really was a good thing he hadn't found Fin at home. Maybe all that Oonagh had been telling him was nothing but the truth!

'And is it special teeth they all have in Fin's family?' asked Cucullin at last, nursing his own jaw. His mouth was too sore for any more bacon and cabbage.

'Would you like to feel for yourself?' answered Oonagh. 'I'll get the little fellow to open his mouth for you. But perhaps you'd be afraid of him? It's rather far back in his mouth his teeth are – just put in your longest finger!'

Well, can you guess now what happened? Indeed perhaps you'd hardly believe it, if you didn't know already that there's hardly an end to the foolishness of giants. Yes, that was it!

Cucullin, with a little bit of help from Oonagh, was

so foolish as to put in that one special finger of his, the middle finger of his right hand, right into Fin's mouth! Well, maybe Fin wasn't the bravest or the wisest, but all the same he was wise enough to give a good hard bite when he had such a chance as that! So now there stood Cucullin without his finger, and worse than that, without his strength. So at last, Fin plucked up his courage, jumped out of the cradle and then Cucullin thought best to run for it.

Away and away, all down Knockmany Hill Fin chased him, for if Cucullin's strength was gone, he could still run. So at last, since he couldn't catch him Fin came back, and by then Oonagh had taken the griddles out of the loaves. So the two of them sat down in peace to eat what was left of the dinner that clever Oonagh had set for Cucullin.

Mrs Pepperpot Buys Macaroni

'It's a very long time since we've had macaroni for supper,' said Mr Pepperpot one day.

'Then you shall have it today, my love,' said his wife. 'But I shall have to go to the grocer for some. So first of all you'll have to find me.'

'Find you?' said Mr Pepperpot. 'What sort of nonsense is that?' But when he looked round for her he couldn't see her anywhere. 'Don't be silly, wife,' he said; 'if you're hiding in the cupboard you must come out this minute. We're too big to play hide-and-seek.'

'I'm not too big, I'm just the right size for "hunt-the-pepperpot",' laughed Mrs Pepperpot. 'Find me if you can!'

'I'm not going to charge round my own bedroom looking for my wife,' he said crossly.

'Now, now! I'll help you; I'll tell you when you're warm. Just now you're very cold.' For Mr Pepperpot was peering out of the window, thinking she might have jumped out. As he searched round the room she called out 'Warm!', 'Colder!', 'Getting hotter!'

until he was quite dizzy.

At last she shouted, 'You'll burn the top of your bald head if you don't look up!' And there she was, sitting on the bed post, swinging her legs and laughing at him.

Her husband pulled a very long face when he saw her.

'This is a bad business – a very bad business,' he said, stroking her cheek with his little finger.

'I don't think it's a bad business,' said Mrs Pepperpot.

'I shall have a terrible time. The whole town will laugh when they see I have a wife the size of a pepperpot.'

'Who cares?' she answered. 'That doesn't matter a bit. Now put me down on the floor so that I can get ready to go to the grocer and buy your macaroni.'

But her husband wouldn't hear of her going; he would go to the grocer himself.

'That'll be a lot of use!' she said. 'When you get home you'll have forgotten to buy the macaroni. I'm sure even if I wrote "macaroni" right across your forehead you'd bring back cinnamon and salt herrings instead.'

'But how are you going to walk all that way with those tiny legs?'

'Put me in your coat pocket; then I won't need to walk.'

There was no help for it, so Mr Pepperpot put his wife in his pocket and set off for the shop.

Soon she started talking: 'My goodness me, what a lot of strange things you have in your pocket – screws and nails, tobacco and matches – there's even a fish-hook! You'll have to take that out at once; I might get it caught in my skirt.'

'Don't talk so loud,' said her husband as he took out the fish-hook. 'We're going into the shop now.'

It was an old-fashioned village store where they sold everything from prunes to coffee cups. The grocer was particularly proud of the coffee cups and held one up for Mr Pepperpot to see. This made his wife curious and she popped her head out of his pocket.

'You stay where you are!' whispered Mr Pepperpot.

'I beg your pardon, did you say anything?' asked the grocer.

'No, no, I was just humming a little tune,' said Mr Pepperpot. 'Tra-la-la!'

'What colour are the cups?' whispered his wife. And her husband sang:

> 'The cups are blue
> With gold edge too,
> But they cost too much
> So that won't do!'

After that Mrs Pepperpot kept quiet – but not for long. When her husband pulled out his tobacco tin she couldn't resist hanging on to the lid. Neither her

28

husband nor anyone else in the shop noticed her slipping on to the counter and hiding behind a flour-bag. From there she darted silently across to the scales, crawled under them, past a pair of kippers wrapped in newspaper, and found herself next to the coffee cups.

'Aren't they pretty!' she whispered, and took a step backwards to get a better view. Whoops! She fell right into the macaroni drawer which had been left open. She hastily covered herself up with macaroni, but the grocer heard the scratching noise and quickly banged the drawer shut. You see, it did sometimes happen that mice got in the drawers, and that's not the sort of thing you want people to know

about, so the grocer pretended nothing had happened and went on serving.

There was Mrs Pepperpot all in the dark; she could hear the grocer serving her husband now. 'That's good,' she thought. 'When he orders macaroni I'll get my chance to slip into the bag with it.'

But it was just as she had feared; her husband forgot what he had come to buy. Mrs Pepperpot shouted at the top of her voice, 'MACARONI!', but it was impossible to get him to hear.

'A quarter of a pound of coffee, please,' said her husband.

'Anything else?' asked the grocer.

'MACARONI!' shouted Mrs Pepperpot.

'Two pounds of sugar,' said her husband.

'Anything more?'

'MACARONI!' shouted Mrs Pepperpot.

But at last her husband remembered the macaroni of his own accord. The grocer hurriedly filled a bag. He thought he felt something move, but he didn't say a word.

'That's all, thank you,' said Mr Pepperpot. When he got outside the door he was just about to make sure his wife was still in his pocket when a van drew up and offered to give him a lift all the way home. Once there he took off his knapsack with all the shopping in it and put his hand in his pocket to lift out his wife.

The pocket was empty.

Now he was really frightened. First he thought she

was teasing him, but when he had called three times and still no wife appeared, he put on his hat again and hurried back to the shop.

The grocer saw him coming. 'He's probably going to complain about the mouse in the macaroni,' he thought.

'Have you forgotten anything, Mr Pepperpot?' he asked, and smiled as pleasantly as he could.

Mr Pepperpot was looking all round. 'Yes,' he said.

'I would be very grateful, Mr Pepperpot, if you would keep it to yourself about the mouse being in the macaroni. I'll let you have these fine blue coffee cups if you'll say no more about it.'

'Mouse?' Mr Pepperpot looked puzzled.

'Shh!' said the grocer, and hurriedly started wrapping up the cups.

Then Mr Pepperpot realized that the grocer had mistaken his wife for a mouse. So he took the cups and rushed home as fast as he could. By the time he got there he was in a sweat of fear that his wife might have been squeezed to death in the macaroni bag.

'Oh, my dear wife,' he muttered to himself. 'My poor darling wife. I'll never again be ashamed of you being the size of a pepperpot – as long as you're still alive!'

When he opened the door she was standing by the cooking-stove, dishing up the macaroni – as large as life; in fact, as large as you or I.

The Emperor's Oblong Pancake

Long, long ago in the East there was an Emperor
who loved pancakes. Every day of the year he had
six pancakes for breakfast; great, big yellow ones they
were, and a little bit brown on top; in fact, just done
to a turn.

And, of course, they were round; as round as
round as round.

One fine morning in spring, when all the almond
trees in the palace courtyard were bursting into
blossom, the Emperor came down to breakfast feeling
especially merry. You see, it was his birthday.

'Happy Birthday, your Excellency,' said the first
footman, as the Emperor sat down at the breakfast
table, and he pushed the Emperor's chair up snug
behind his knees.

'Happy Birthday, your Excellency,' said the second
footman, as he laid out the Emperor's golden spoon,
fork and knife in front of him.

'Happy Birthday, your Excellency,' said the third
footman, helping to tuck the Emperor's gleaming
white napkin into his red velvet collar, and spreading

it neatly over his gold-embroidered waistcoat.

'Happy Birthday, your Excellency,' said the Court Chamberlain as he bowed low. Then he beckoned forward the first footman again, bearing a huge golden bowl full of hot, steaming porridge.

'And the same to you,' said the Emperor, merrily, as he shook the sugar and poured the cream; and with that he set briskly to work, opening all his birthday cards with his left hand, and scooping porridge into his mouth with his right, as merry as merry could be.

In no time at all the Emperor's porridge was finished, and all his birthday cards were propped up in front of him. Immediately the third footman whisked away the empty plate, and the Court Chamberlain marched solemnly to the door, where he took up the big gong stick, made of solid ebony, and beat the big gong, made of solid brass. This was the signal for the fourth and fifth footmen to bring in the main dish.

At the far end of the dining room the big bronze doors flew open, and in came the fourth and fifth footmen, bearing between them a broad silver dish with a broad silver dish cover. Up the length of the dining room they marched, with the Court Chamberlain walking in front, carrying his wand of office until they reached the Emperor.

The fourth and fifth footmen bowed as low as low. 'Happy Birthday, your Excellency,' they cried together.

'And the same to you,' beamed the Emperor, still as merry as ever, and he rubbed his hands together in anticipation, as the fourth and fifth footmen took the cover off the silver dish.

'Pancakes!' cried the Emperor. 'How very nice! Capital!' just as if he didn't have pancakes every day of the year.

Then the fourth and fifth footmen, armed with huge silver forks, began carefully lifting the pancakes from the silver dish, one by one, and laying them on the Emperor's golden plate. Pale yellow, they were, and slightly, ever so slightly brown on top; in fact, just done to a turn; and, of course, they were all as round as round as round.

Out they came, one, two, three, four, five, and each as round and crisp as could be.

And now, as the Emperor reached for the sugar, out came the last pancake. Clang went the silver cover on the silver dish, and the Emperor was just about to dig in, when he stopped.

He stopped and he stared! He stopped and he stared and he gasped!

Then, trembling with fury, he rose slowly to his feet. His face began to turn bright purple, and he tore his white dinner napkin out of his red velvet collar and flung it across the room. Then he opened his mouth and roared.

And what he roared was: 'OBLONG!'

Everybody stared in horror, and everybody trembled in fear. Then the five footmen, terrified out of

their wits, turned tail and fled through the great
bronze doors, which clanged shut behind them.

The Court Chamberlain had half a mind to follow
them; but then he remembered that before being
Court Chamberlain, he had been the bravest corporal
in the Emperor's army. So he stood his ground.

'Excellency,' said the Court Chamberlain, bowing
right down to the ground, and raising his eyebrows
at the same time.

'Oblong!' roared the Emperor again; then he

35

stabbed with his fork, plonk right into the middle of the sixth pancake, and raised it high in the air like a flag.

'It's an insult!' he shouted. 'This pancake is oblong!'

And so it was; as oblong as oblong as oblong.

The Chamberlain stared at the pancake and the Emperor stared at the Chamberlain.

'Explain!' he roared.

'I . . . I can't, your Excellency,' stammered the Chamberlain. 'That is, not just at the moment. However, I'll find out about it immediately, immediately, Excellency,' and with a somewhat hasty bow he hurried away down the long, marble dining room and out through the bronze double doors.

Left to himself, the Emperor began to feel rather foolish, standing there holding his fork aloft with the oblong pancake dangling from it. Besides, the other five pancakes looked all right. They smelled very nice too, and after all it was his birthday, and he was still hungry.

'Drat the thing!' said the Emperor, and stepping smartly over to the window he hurled the offending pancake as far as he could. Out across the courtyard it flew, and stuck in the top of one of the almond trees, sending a shower of pale pink almond blossoms whirling down on to the marble pavement.

By and by the Emperor finished the five round pancakes, and he was just having an extra piece of toast to make up for the one pancake he hadn't had, when the bronze double doors flew open and the Court Chamberlain hurried in.

He was relieved to find the Emperor looking fairly calm again, and advancing up the long carpet, he bowed low.

'Excellency,' he began.

'Well,' said the Emperor, rather indistinctly through the toast.

'Excellency, it would appear it was a birthday present.'

'A what?' asked the Emperor, a good deal surprised.

'Well, actually, Excellency, and in point of fact,' said the Chamberlain, bowing till his forehead touched his shoes, 'it was the frying pan.'

Then the Emperor began to smile. 'I think I see,' he said. 'The frying pan was a birthday present, and being oblong, it fried an oblong pancake.'

The Court Chamberlain straightened up sharply. 'Your Excellency's perspicacity is indeed remarkable,' he said.

'Oh, I don't know,' said the Emperor, modestly, and in fact he didn't, but it sounded complimentary, and he was pleased to have guessed right.

He walked slowly back to his chair, and sat musing a while, twiddling the sugar spoon.

'You know,' he said, slowly, 'I rather like the idea. An oblong frying pan, eh? Oblong pancakes, what? Yes, I certainly like the idea. After all,' he added, 'one likes to be a little different, doesn't one?'

37

The Court Chamberlain was vastly relieved. 'Of course, Excellency, exactly,' he said. 'Oh, yes indeed!'

'Good!' said the Emperor. 'Then that's understood, oblong pancakes only in future.' And with that he bounced away out of the dining room, as merry as ever, to see to the day's business.

Now that, you might think, was the end of the story. So, indeed, it would have been if this had been an ordinary Emperor; but he wasn't; and he soon made up his mind that everyone in the Empire should share his great discovery. In no time at all the whole population was buying oblong frying pans and frying oblong pancakes; and those who were too poor to buy new ones took hammers or stones or lumps of wood and banged their round frying pans oblong. The Emperor had ordered it, and that was that.

As for the Emperor, he was still as merry as ever, and very pleased with himself for having had such an original idea. For by this time he was quite persuaded he had thought the whole thing out himself. He was still as merry as ever, until one morning in autumn, when the leaves of the almond trees in the courtyard were beginning to turn brown.

On that particular morning the Emperor was just finishing his sixth pancake when an uneasy feeling came over him.

Oblong pancakes, undoubtedly, were the only thing for a man of sense; but something still seemed not quite as it should be. The Emperor pondered, staring at his empty plate; and as he stared he began to smile.

'Of course,' he murmured, 'why didn't I think of it before? Oblong pancakes need oblong plates. It's common sense.' Springing to his feet, he strode across the marble dining room and tugged the bell-pull.

Down in the butler's pantry the Court Chamberlain was just going to start his own oblong pancake when the bell jangled so hard it nearly fell off the wall. Dropping his fork with a clatter, the Chamberlain seized his wand of office and rushed up the marble stairs and through the bronze double doors into the Emperor's dining room. There he bowed low before the Emperor.

'Excellency?' said the Chamberlain, rather out of breath.

'Oblong pancakes need oblong plates,' said the Emperor, briefly. 'Arrange it.'

'Excellency,' said the Court Chamberlain, bowing again. And by breakfast-time the next morning, there before the Emperor was a fine golden plate, all new and gleaming, with the imperial arms stamped in the middle. Of course it was oblong.

The Emperor said nothing, but he was pleased all the same. He liked to have his orders promptly obeyed, and besides, one did like to be just a little different.

Of course the Emperor didn't stay different very long, because he soon had every potter and tinsmith in the Empire turning out oblong plates for every man, woman and child in the land. He was so proud of his good idea and besides he was not a selfish man.

But by the end of a week the Emperor was worrying again. He had a tidy mind, and it bothered him to see oblong plates on the table mixed up with cups and saucers which were round. They didn't match. So – you've guessed it – the necessary orders were given, and in no time at all oblong cups and saucers were the rule throughout the country.

By this time the whole idea was beginning to become an obsession. Once started, the Emperor found himself unable to stop, and soon he was ordering something round to be changed to oblong every day.

As for the people, they knew what the Emperor was like when he got hold of an idea, and they soon began to guess what he would change next. Without waiting to be told, they began to throw out everything in their houses which was round, and to have everything oblong instead.

They had oblong saucepans, and oblong spoons and oblong bottles and oblong dishes. They ate oblong pies and oblong tarts and oblong cheeses. They wore oblong hats and they carried oblong umbrellas when it rained. They even bumped about the streets in carriages with oblong wheels. Oh, it was most uncomfortable, but the Emperor was bound to order it sooner or later, and he liked things done so fast, it was best to be prepared.

The Emperor soon learned how the people were so loyal that they tried to anticipate his every wish. But at the same time he couldn't help trying to think of new things to change before they did; and before long he began to order really difficult things like oblong apples and oblong eggs. He was the Emperor, of course, and however difficult it might be, his order must be obeyed. All the farmers and gardeners and all the scientists and professors set to work to see that they were . . . and by the next autumn all the apple trees were loaded with oblong apples, and all the pear trees with oblong pears; and all the hens in the land, poor things, were laying oblong eggs like anything. Even the almonds on the almond trees in the palace courtyard were oblong, and as the Emperor surveyed the scene from his dining room window, he was filled with pride by his own quick thinking and the cleverness of his subjects.

What other monarch, he mused, could have achieved so much in so short a time? He stood there at the window, his hands clasped behind his back, puffing out his chest and surveying the scene with great satisfaction.

Among the oblong almonds the blue and green parakeets flitted and chattered; the fountains splashed gently in their oblong pools; ranged along the far side of the courtyard stood the Emperor's great brass cannons, each with its pile of oblong cannon-balls, and over all shone the soft, warm radiance of

41

the autumn sun.

'What a beautiful day,' sighed the Emperor contentedly, gazing up at the cloudless blue sky. 'What a beautiful, beautiful d . . .'

> *And then he stopped.*
> *He stopped and he stared.*
> *He stopped and he stared and he gasped.*
> *Then he opened his mouth and roared.*
> *And what he roared was: 'ROUND!'*

The Court Chamberlain was just putting all the knives and forks and oblong spoons into the silver box marked 'Cutlery' when the Emperor roared 'ROUND!' and the clatter was dreadful as they flew in all directions over the marble floor.

Pulling himself together, the Court Chamberlain bent low, raising his eyebrows at the same time.

'Excellency?'

'ROUND!' roared the Emperor again. 'The sun is round! Have it changed at once!'

'The sun, Excellency?' stammered the Chamberlain, unable to believe his ears.

'Yes, you fool, the sun!' bellowed the Emperor, fairly dancing with rage. 'That ugly, great, yellow, round thing hanging over my lovely oblong empire. It's ruining everything. Change it!'

The Court Chamberlain didn't dare to argue. He knew what the Emperor was like when his mind was made up. So, although he hadn't the slightest idea what he was going to do, 'Yes, Excellency,' he said, and he bolted out through the bronze double doors.

Once outside, the Chamberlain stopped, pulled out a large red spotted handkerchief and, leaning against a pillar, mopped his brow.

The sun! How in the name of all that was round could anybody make the sun oblong? It was too far away for one thing, and for another it was much too hot.

The Court Chamberlain opened the bronze doors a crack and peeped through. There was the Emperor, still fuming up and down in front of the window, and glaring up at the sun every few seconds, obviously expecting it to turn oblong any moment.

The Chamberlain shut the door, shrugged his shoulders hopelessly, and went off to try.

First he told all the Emperor's woodmen to chop down every tree in the Empire, and then he told all the Emperor's soldiers to build them up into a tall, tall tower, just outside the palace walls.

Every day the tower grew taller, and every day the Chamberlain climbed to the top to see if they were getting anywhere near the sun yet.

By and by there were no more trees left, and the sun seemed as far as ever, so they gave that up.

Then the Chamberlain asked all the Emperor's soldiers if any of them would volunteer to be tied to one of the Emperor's oblong cannonballs and be shot up to the sun with a hammer in his hand. At first none of them would, but at last one of the very

43

bravest said he would try. So they tied him firmly by the middle to an oblong cannonball, and put a heavy hammer in his hand. The Chamberlain told him exactly what to do when he reached the sun, and then they shut their eyes and shot him off.

Up he went like a rocket, but as he was rather fat he didn't go nearly high enough, and he soon came down again and stuck in the top of one of the almond trees in the courtyard; and then he fell out of the tree and splash into one of the oblong fountain pools. A very sorry sight he looked by the time the rest of them hauled him out. Still, they gave him a medal for trying, and the Chamberlain thought again.

He was just working out a method of throwing a stone into the sky without letting go of it, when finally the Emperor lost patience.

He rang all the bells in the palace very loudly, and the Chamberlain and the five footmen and the soldiers, and all the lords and ladies of the court besides, not to mention the people, hurried into the palace courtyard. The Emperor addressed them from the balcony.

'You are the most useless lot of subjects an Emperor ever had,' he said crossly. 'You don't deserve a progressive monarch like myself. I gave orders three weeks ago for the sun to be made oblong, and look at it – still as round as round as round – horrible!' and the Emperor shuddered.

'We have done our best, Excellency,' ventured the Court Chamberlain.

'We've tried and tried and tried,' cried all the Emperor's soldiers and the five footmen. All the lords and ladies nodded in agreement, though what they had done goodness only knew.

'Your best is not good enough,' said the Emperor, crossly. 'You all deserve to be boiled in oil. Instead, however . . .', he paused and surveyed them disdainfully, '. . . instead, however, I shall do the job myself.

'Do you not know,' he went on, 'that every evening the sun comes down to the edge of the earth? That is the time to deal with it.' Then turning to the Court Chamberlain, he said, 'Bring out my chariot.'

The Chamberlain gave a signal, and the Sergeant-of-Horse led out the chariot, with four black horses dancing and prancing and kicking up the dust, and the Emperor climbed aboard.

They handed him a large packet of dried dates and a parcel of ready cooked pancakes for the journey, and also a pair of blacksmith's tongs and a heavy hammer, which the Emperor stowed under the seat.

Then, pressing his crown firmly on his head, he whipped up the horses, and shot away in a huge cloud of dust.

The people watched the dust cloud grow smaller in the distance until it dwindled out of sight. Then they all went home.

The next morning everyone was up early to see the sunrise. As the first pink glow appeared in the east, all the domes of the palace, and all the roofs in

45

the town were crowded with onlookers. The pink turned to orange, and then to bright yellow, and all the people craned their necks and held their breath.

Then, suddenly, up popped the sun and all the people groaned. It was still as round as round.

'It must be further than we thought,' said the Chamberlain. 'No wonder we never reached it with the tower. Still, the Emperor is so determined, he is sure to get there in the end. We shall have to be patient and wait.'

So they did. But while they waited, the days grew into weeks and the weeks grew to months, and still the sun came up every morning as round as ever.

Meanwhile, however, some of the people, less patient than the others, began to get tired of bumping about in carriages and carts with oblong wheels. It was really very inconvenient; and so, one by one, they began to change all their oblong wheels back to round ones again. However, they all knew that what they had done was against the Emperor's wishes, so they all pretended not to notice what had happened.

And then, one day, quite suddenly, very much to everyone's surprise, and his own as well, the Emperor came back.

'Well I never!' said the Emperor, climbing stiffly out of his chariot. Everybody stared, and said, 'Well I never!' too.

'I must have taken a wrong turning somewhere,' went on the Emperor, feeling rather foolish. 'How very, very annoying!'

So the Chamberlain arranged for the Emperor to have a wash and brush up and a little something to keep out the cold; and they stocked up the chariot again with food for the journey. Then, amid the cheers of all the people, the Emperor drove away to the west once more, and vanished over the horizon.

Again the days passed, and the weeks as well, but still the sun was as round as round; and not only the sun. I am afraid the people started to change other things besides the carriage wheels. It was a great strain on all the hens to keep laying oblong eggs, so they were allowed to go back to laying round ones; and of course that meant changing back all the egg cups as well. They were beginning to change the egg spoons too, when the Emperor suddenly came back again.

'Oh, bother!' said the Emperor, jumping crossly from his chariot. 'I seem to have gone wrong again.' But he was very determined, as you know by now, and he wouldn't give up. However, just to see what happened, this time he pointed his chariot the other way, and galloped rapidly away towards the east. Immediately everyone went back to changing the spoons, and because the gardeners had forgotten to use the special fertilizer, all the fruit trees began to produce ordinary, round apples and oranges and pears and almonds once more.

And so it went on for a long while. The sun stayed as round as round, and gradually everything in the Empire which had once been oblong was changed to being round too. Every now and then the Emperor would suddenly arrive back again, and say 'Oh, bother!' and gallop off in a new direction.

But as time passed it became clear that no matter in which direction he galloped, he always came back again to where he had started from. No one could understand it.

Then one day in spring, when the almond trees in the palace courtyard were bursting into blossom, the Emperor came back for the umpteenth time; but this time he didn't say, 'Oh, bother!' Instead he came galloping up as merry as could be, and bounced out of his chariot and up the marble staircase into the palace.

Then he rang all the bells, and summoned the people into the courtyard.

Soon they were assembled, but they held their hats behind their backs, because, of course, they were all round, and they didn't want the Emperor to see. The Sergeant of the Guard had sentries stationed in front of the cannons, so as to hide the piles of round cannonballs from the Emperor.

The Emperor, looking very pleased with himself, stepped out on to the balcony, and addressed them.

'My people,' he began, 'you have been very patient. I have been away a long time, and you have remained loyal and obedient subjects in every way. I am very pleased with you all.'

At this the people cheered, but they felt a little nervous, and no one more so than the Chamberlain.

He could not help remembering all the things which had been changed from oblong to round against the Emperor's wishes.

But the Emperor was speaking again.

'My people,' he said, 'I have failed to reach the sun; but . . .' and he began to smile broadly, and puffed out his chest till all his decorations rattled and the buttons nearly flew off his waistcoat. 'It no longer matters. Changing the sun is a very minor matter, after all, compared with the remarkable discovery I have made. My people,' said the Emperor, proudly, 'my dear people, your Emperor has established by personal experiment, and beyond all reasonable doubt, a new and amazing scientific fact. The world, in short. . . . THE WORLD IS ROUND!'

You should have heard the cheering. The people cheered, and the soldiers cheered, the footmen cheered, the lords and ladies cheered; and none cheered louder than the Chamberlain.

The Emperor bowed and smiled, and smiled and bowed, and then he held his hand up again.

'The world is round, my people, as round as round as round. And very nice, too. So now, in consequence, it is my wish that everything in the Empire should be round as well – to match.'

The Court Chamberlain stepped forward and bowed as low as low: 'Your Excellency,' he said, 'may it please your Excellency, it is already done.'

The Emperor was so pleased at this that he danced a little jig, clapping his hands and crying 'Capital,

capital, capital!'

Then the Emperor turned and entered the marble dining room, followed by the Chamberlain and the five footmen.

'Now,' said the Emperor, rubbing his hands, 'what about breakfast?'

'May I suggest pancakes, your Excellency?' ventured the Court Chamberlain with a smile.

'Excellent!' said the Emperor. 'Nothing could be nicer.'

'Would your Excellency prefer them round or – or – oblong?' inquired the Chamberlain, bowing as low as low.

The Emperor thought for a moment, rubbing his chin, and then his eyes twinkled, and he said: 'Oblong, please. I shall continue to have my pancakes oblong. After all the frying pan was a birthday present, and I wouldn't like to hurt anyone's feelings. And besides,' finished the Emperor, settling comfortably in his chair, 'besides, one does like to be a little different after all!'

Big Claus and Little Claus

Once upon a time there were two men who lived in the same town and had the same name – both were called Claus. But one of them had four horses and the other only one. So to tell one from the other, they called the one who owned four horses Big Claus and the one who owned only one horse Little Claus. And now let's find out how these two got on together, for it really is quite a story.

For six days of the week Little Claus had to do the ploughing for Big Claus and lend him his one horse. In return Big Claus would help Little Claus with his four horses – but only once a week, on Sundays. And how Little Claus would crack down his whip on all five horses on Sundays, when the horses were his! The sun would shine so bright, the bells in the church would peal out loud and clear and people would walk by in their very best clothes with their hymn-books under their arms, on their way to hear the vicar preach his sermon, and they would see Little Claus ploughing away with five horses. And he would feel so happy that he would bring down his whip with a resounding thwack! and cry: 'Gee-up there, all my horses.'

'Don't SAY that,' warned Big Claus. 'Only one of them is yours.'

But as soon as anyone passed by again on the way to church, Little Claus would forget about this and he would cry out: 'Gee-up there, all my horses.'

'Now stop that at once, if you please,' warned Big Claus again. 'If you say it just once more, I'll crack your horse over the head and kill him dead; and that'll be the end of him.'

'I won't say it again, I promise,' said Little Claus. But when the people walked by and nodded Good-day he would feel so happy and so grand to have five horses that he would crack his whip and cry out, 'Gee-up there, all my horses!'

'I'll teach you to gee-up your horses,' said Big Claus and, taking a mallet, he brought down such a mighty crack on the head of Little Claus's only horse that it fell down dead on the spot.

'Oh dear,' wailed Little Claus. 'Now I haven't got a horse at all.' And he started to cry. But he didn't cry for very long. He stripped the hide off his dead horse and then left the hide to dry in the wind. Then he put it into a bag, threw the bag over his shoulders and set off to sell the horse-hide in the nearest town.

It was a very long way, through a great dark wood, and all of a sudden there was a terrible storm. Little Claus was quite lost and wandered all over the place until at last he found himself outside a large farmhouse. The shutters were up, for it was already night-fall, but he could see a small light shining over the top of them.

'I expect they will put me up for the night,' thought Little Claus and he went and knocked at the door.

The farmer's wife opened it. When she heard what he wanted she said: 'You can't come in here. My husband is away and I don't take strangers in.' And with that she shut the door in his face.

Little Claus looked around. There was a haystack close by and between that and the farmhouse there was a shed with a flat thatched roof.

'I can sleep up there,' thought Little Claus, looking up at the roof. 'It should make a fine bed. I don't imagine that stork will fly down and peck my legs' (for, standing on the roof, was a real stork which had built its nest there).

So up he climbed on to the shed and lay down and wriggled about till he was nice and comfortable. The shutters on the farmhouse windows did not quite fit at the top, so he was able to look over them, right inside, and see what was going on.

He could see a big table spread with roast meat and red wine and some very tasty-looking fish. The farmer's wife and the village schoolmaster were sitting there and she was filling up his glass and he was helping himself to the fish, to which he seemed to be very partial.

'Wouldn't I just like to have some of that!' thought Little Claus, sticking his head as close to the window as he could. 'Goodness me, what a splendid cake! What a feast they're having!'

Just then he heard the sound of horses' hooves along the high road. They were coming towards the house; it was the woman's husband coming home. He was a most worthy man but he had one rather strange weakness – he couldn't stand the sight of village schoolmasters. The mere mention of one would send him mad with rage, which was why the schoolmaster was visiting the farmer's wife when her husband was away and why she was now offering him her tastiest dishes. So now, when they heard her husband coming, they both got very frightened and the woman told the schoolmaster to hide in a large empty chest in the corner. Which he did at once, and the woman quickly put away all the delicious food and wine in her oven, for if her husband had seen them he would certainly have asked what it all meant.

'Oh, what a shame,' sighed Little Claus from his thatched bed, when he saw all the appetizing food disappear into the oven.

'Who is that up there?' called the farmer, looking up at Little Claus. 'Why are you lying there? Come indoors with me.'

Little Claus then told him about the storm and how he had lost his way and asked the good farmer if he could put him up for the night.

'Most certainly,' said the farmer, 'but first let's have a bite of supper.'

The farmer's wife had now become all friendly and welcomed Little Claus when she saw him at the door with her husband. She spread the cloth on the long table and served them a large bowl of porridge. The farmer ate heartily enough but Little Claus could not take his mind off the delicious roast meat and fish and the wine and the cake which he knew were in the oven. Under the table at his feet was the bag with the horse-hide. He trod on the bag and the dry hide gave out a loud squeak.

'Hush!' said Little Claus pretending to listen to something, and he trod on it again, making it squeak even louder.

'Hullo,' said the farmer, 'what's that you've got under there?'

'Oh, that's my wizard. I keep him in my bag,' replied Little Claus. 'He says we are not to eat the porridge for he's conjured the whole oven full of roast meat, fish, cake and red wine.'

'What! What!' exclaimed the farmer, and stretching over to the oven, he opened it and saw all the delicious food his wife had hidden away there but which he believed the wizard had conjured up for him.

His wife, not daring to say a word, placed all the food on the table at once and they helped themselves freely. When they had eaten and drunk to their hearts' content, the farmer became quite jolly and asked: 'What else can your wizard do? Can he call up the Devil, I wonder? I'd like to see him do that.'

'Oh yes,' said Little Claus, 'my wizard will do anything I ask – won't you?' and he trod on his bag again. 'Did you hear him say "yes"? But the Devil is not very pretty to look at and I shouldn't bother to see him if I were you.'

'Oh, I'm not afraid,' said the farmer. 'What does he really look like?'

'Well, as far as I know, he may well show himself looking like a village schoolmaster.'

'Ugh!' grunted the farmer with a start, 'I can't stand the sight of village schoolmasters. But, no matter, as long as I know it's the Devil I shan't mind. I'm quite brave – but don't let him come too near me, mind.'

'I'll ask my wizard then,' said Little Claus, and he trod on his bag and bent down to listen.

'What does he say?' asked the farmer.

'He says: "Go over to that chest in the corner and you'll find the Devil crouching inside." But hold the lid firm so that he doesn't slip out.'

The farmer went over to the chest, lifted the lid and peeped inside.

'Ugh!' he shrieked and shrank back. 'He looks the very image of our village schoolmaster. What a horrid sight!' And then they drank some more wine to get over the shock, and in fact they went on drinking all through the night.

'You know, you'll have to sell me that wizard of yours,' said the farmer. 'I'll pay you as much as you like – a whole bushel of money, just say the word.'

'Oh no!' said Little Claus. 'Just think of all the things he can do for me.'

'Oh please,' begged the farmer, 'I simply must have that wizard. I'd give anything in the world for him.'

'Oh very well then,' said Little Claus. 'As you've been kind enough to give me a night's lodging, you can have my wizard for a bushel of money, but I insist on a full measure.'

'Of course,' said the farmer, 'but see that that chest is taken away. I won't have it in my home one moment longer. He may still be inside,' he added with a shudder.

Little Claus gave the farmer his bag with the dry horse-hide and in return received a whole bushel of money, full measure. The farmer also gave him a wheelbarrow to wheel away the money and the chest.

'Good-bye,' said Little Claus and off he went, wheeling the barrow with the bushel of money and the chest (with the village schoolmaster inside).

He reached the other side of the forest where there was a deep, swiftly flowing river. A fine new bridge had been built across it and when he was about half-way across, Little Claus said, loud enough for the schoolmaster to hear: 'Now what am I to do with this silly old chest? It's no use to me. I'd better heave it into the river and get rid of it.' And he took hold of one end and lifted it up a bit.

'No, stop!' cried the village schoolmaster from inside the chest. 'Let me out! Let me out!'

'Ugh!' cried Little Claus, pretending to be scared. 'He's still there! I'd better drop it straight into the river and drown him before he gets out.'

'Oh no!' pleaded the village schoolmaster. 'Let me out and I'll give you a whole bushel of money.'

'Well, that's different,' said Little Claus, opening the chest and letting out the village schoolmaster. Little Claus pushed the chest into the river and the schoolmaster ran home and came back to give Little Claus another whole bushel of money.

'I seem to have got a pretty good price for that horse of mine,' he said to himself when he got home and counted out his two bushels of money. 'Big Claus will be none too pleased when he finds out how rich I've grown from my one horse.'

Soon after this he sent a boy over to Big Claus to borrow a bushel measure. 'What on earth can he want that for?' wondered Big Claus, and he stuck a bit of tar at the bottom of it so that whatever Little Claus was measuring would stick to it. And indeed that is just what did happen. For when the measure was returned to Big Claus there were two gleaming silver florins sticking to it.

'What does this mean?' said Big Claus and he dashed straight off to Little Claus and asked, 'Where have you got all this money from?'

'Oh, that's from the horse-hide which I sold yesterday.'

'And a handsome price you must have got for it,' said Big Claus. And he hurried back home, took an axe and struck all his four horses down dead. Then he stripped their skins off and drove off to town with them.

'Skins, horses' skins! Who'll buy my skins?' he shouted as he went through the streets. All the tanners and shoemakers came out and asked what price he was asking.

'A bushel of money per piece,' he replied.

'A bushel of money!' they all cried in amazement. 'Are you mad? D'you think we are fools?' And they took their straps and leather aprons and began to beat him and thrash him until he was chased right out of town. When he got back home that night he was very angry. 'Little Claus will pay for this,' he kept muttering. 'He'll pay with his life for this. I'll kill him.'

Just about this time Little Claus's grandmother died. It's true she hadn't been very kind to him (at times she had even been quite nasty), but he felt very sorry all the same and so he took the dead lady over into his own warm bed to see if he could bring her back to life again. He left her there all night and he went and slept in a chair in a corner of the room.

In the middle of the night the door opened and in crept Big Claus with his axe. He made straight for the bed and hit the dead grandmother on the head, thinking it was Little Claus.

'Well, that's finished him,' he muttered to himself, 'he won't make a fool of me again.' And he went off home.

'Well, well,' said Little Claus. 'What a nasty, wicked man. He meant that blow with the axe for me. It's a good thing old grandmother was dead already or he'd have well and truly done the job himself.'

He then dressed his granny in her Sunday best, borrowed a horse and cart from a neighbour and propped the old lady up on the back seat so that she wouldn't slump out if he drove too fast. Then he started out through the forest. He reached an inn just about sunrise and went inside to have a bite of something to eat.

Mine host the innkeeper was a very rich and very pleasant man on the whole, but there were times when he could get very peppery and lose his temper completely.

'Good morning,' he said to Little Claus. 'I see you're out early today, and in your best clothes too.'

'Yes,' said Little Claus, 'I'm off to town with my grandmother. She's sitting out there in the back seat of the cart. She won't come in, so would you kindly take her out a glass of mead. And speak up loud, won't you, as her hearing is not all that good.'

The innkeeper went out to her. 'Here's a glass of mead from your grandson, madam,' he said.

The dead lady said never a word and sat quite still.

'Can't you hear?' shouted the innkeeper at the top of his voice. 'Here's a glass of mead from your grandson!' He shouted the same thing again and again and as she didn't stir he flew into a rage, completely lost his temper and threw the glass right in the dead lady's face. The mead ran down all over her cheeks and nose and she slumped over the side of the cart – for Little Claus had only propped her up and not tied her fast.

'Now look what you've done!' shouted Little Claus, rushing out of the inn. 'You've killed my poor grandmother. Just look at that great cut in her forehead.'

61

'Oh, what a misfortune!' cried the innkeeper, wringing his hands. 'It's all because of my hot temper. Dear Little Claus! I'll give you a whole bushel of money and have her buried as though she were my own grandmother. Only don't tell anyone, of course, or they'll cut my head off and that wouldn't be at all nice.'

And so Little Claus got another bushel of money and the innkeeper buried the old granny as if she had been his own.

Then Little Claus went back home and sent a boy over to Big Claus to ask if he could borrow a bushel measure.

'My goodness, what can that mean?' wondered Big Claus. 'I killed him, didn't I? I'd better go and see for myself.' So off he went to Little Claus with the bushel measure.

When he saw all the money he gaped with surprise. 'Where did all this come from?' he asked.

'You didn't kill me,' said Little Claus. 'It was my grandmother you killed with your axe. And I've sold her for a bushel of money.'

'My goodness, that's a pretty good price you've got for her,' said Big Claus, and he hurried straight home and killed his grandmother with his axe. Then he put her in a cart and drove to the chemist's and asked him if he wanted to buy a dead body.

'Whose?' asked the chemist. 'And where did you get it?'

'It's my grandmother,' replied Big Claus. 'I've

killed her and I'm asking a bushel of money for her.'

'Heavens above!' cried the chemist. 'What next, I wonder! You must be raving mad. If you go about saying things like that, you'll lose your own head. You're a very wicked man and you deserve to be punished!'

Big Claus got so frightened at this that he rushed out of the shop, jumped into his cart and galloped his horse straight back to his house. The chemist really thought he must have gone mad – and so did everyone else – and they let him drive wherever he wanted to.

Big Claus really was mad – with rage. 'You'll pay for this, Little Claus,' he kept saying. 'You'll most surely pay for this.' And as soon as he was back home, he took the biggest sack he could find and went over to Little Claus and said: 'So you've fooled me again, have you? First, you made me kill my horses and now my grandmother. But you are never going to fool me again!' So saying, he seized Little Claus by the scruff of the neck, put him into the sack and slung the sack over his shoulder. 'And now, Little Claus, I'm going to drown you,' he said.

Little Claus was no lightweight and Big Claus had a long way to go before he got to the river. Along the road they passed a church where they could hear people singing hymns to the accompaniment of a beautiful organ. 'It would be rather nice if I went in and sang a hymn before I go any further,' thought Big Claus, and so he put down his heavy burden and

63

went into the church. 'Oh dear! Oh dear!' Little Claus kept saying as he twisted and turned in the sack; but he couldn't untie the cord. At that moment an old cattle drover was passing, with a big stick in his hand and driving a herd of cows and bullocks. One or two of them stumbled against the sack and knocked it over.

'Oh dear!' sighed Little Claus. 'I'm so very young and I'm going to heaven already.'

'And I'm so very old,' said the drover, 'and I can't get there yet!'

'Open the sack,' cried Little Claus. 'Change places with me and you'll go to heaven straight away!'

'Gladly will I do that,' said the old drover, and he undid the sack and out jumped Little Claus.

'You *will* look after my cattle,' said the drover, getting into the sack.

'To be sure, I will,' said Little Claus, and he tied up the sack and then went off with the cows and bullocks.

Soon Big Claus came out of church and flung the sack over his shoulder, thinking how light it had become – the old drover was less than half the weight of Little Claus. 'He's grown light as a feather,' he muttered to himself. 'It must be the effect of that nice hymn I have sung.' Then he made for the river which was deep and wide, and threw in the sack with the old drover inside.

'Take that, Little Claus,' he shouted, 'you'll not fool me any more.'

He then set off home, but at the crossroads whom should he meet but Little Claus himself, driving his herd of cows and bullocks.

'What does this mean?' asked Big Claus. 'Didn't I just throw you into the river?'

'Yes, you did,' said Little Claus.

'Then where have you got all this cattle from?'

'It's sea-cattle,' said Little Claus. 'I'm very grateful to you for throwing me in, but let me tell you the whole story. I was really terribly frightened when I was tied up inside that sack, and how the wind did howl when you threw me down from the bridge. I went straight to the bottom, of course, only I didn't get hurt because I fell on to the softest of soft grass that grows on the river bed. And then the sack opened and the loveliest of lovely girls in a snow-white dress, with a white garland round her hair, came and took me by the hand and said: "Is that you, Little Claus? Here's some cattle for you, and a mile further along there's another herd for you." I then saw that the river was a wide sea-road for the sea-people. They were walking along down at the bottom, making their way up to the country where the sea ends. I can't tell you how pleasant it was down there, with flowers and green grass, and fishes darting past like birds in the air. And cattle, too, walking along the dikes and ditches.'

'Then whatever made you come up again so soon?' asked Big Claus. 'I would have stayed down much longer, as it seems so very nice down there.'

'Well,' replied Little Claus. 'Listen to me, this will just show you how clever I am. You remember I told you the sea-girl said there was another herd of cattle waiting for me. Well, I know the river winds and bends all over the place so I have decided to make a short cut by coming up on land and then diving down into the river again. I'll save almost half a mile like that, and I'll get the rest of my cattle all the quicker.'

'I must say, you *are* a lucky man,' said Big Claus. 'Do you think I could get some sea-cattle if I went down to the bottom of the river?'

'I don't see why you shouldn't,' replied Little Claus. 'But don't ask me to carry you to the river in a sack, you are far too heavy for me. If you care to walk there and then get into the sack, I'll throw you in with the greatest of pleasure.'

'Thank you very much,' said Big Claus, 'but if I don't get any sea-cattle when I get down there, you can look out! I'll give you the thrashing of your life!'

'Oh please don't be too hard on me,' said Little Claus, and off they went across to the river. When the cattle saw the water they ran towards it as fast as ever they could, for they were very thirsty.

'You can see how eager they are to get to the bottom again,' said Little Claus.

'Yes, yes,' said Big Claus impatiently. 'I can see that, but you've got to help me to get in first or else you'll get that thrashing I promised you.'

'Very well,' said Little Claus, helping Big Claus to

66

get into the sack. 'And put a stone in it in case I don't sink,' added Big Claus as his head disappeared inside the sack.

'You'll sink all right,' said Little Claus. And putting in a large stone, he tied the cord tight and pushed the sack into the flowing water.

'I'm very much afraid he won't get those cattle,' said Little Claus, and he drove off back home with what he had got.

The Wishing-skin

Once upon a time there was a woodcutter whose name was Rudolf. He was very poor, and he lived with his wife in a little hut made of split logs, in the middle of a deep forest.

The forest was so thick that people scarcely ever passed Rudolf's hut. But the woodcutter wasn't lonely. When he was at home he sat by the fire, talking to his wife; and when he was in the woods, he made friends with the birds and the animals. The furry beasts and the little feathered folk used to watch him out of their bright eyes and come quite close to his feet without being afraid. Then Rudolf would look at them and say: 'Good morning, little comrades! I'd rather have friends like you than all the riches in the world.'

One day the King came hunting in the woods, looking for wild deer. Princes and princesses came with him, and lords and ladies too. They came once. They came twice. They came three times. And they liked it so much that after that they came nearly every day.

Their clothes were of velvet edged with fur. They rode fine horses with little silver bells round their necks, and they had servants dressed in green and gold who brought baskets of food for them to eat when they were hungry, and flasks of sparkling wine to drink when they were thirsty.

Sometimes they stopped at Rudolf's little hut and peeped in and laughed, saying: 'See the funny old table with no fine linen! Look, he hasn't any chairs! How quaint! How old-fashioned!' and they would sit on Rudolf's three-legged stools and say: 'Ooh, how hard! He must wear out his breeches without a velvet cushion.' And when they saw the darns and patches in Rudolf's breeches, they laughed and said: 'Ha! Ha! We were right.' When Rudolf heard this he was ashamed of his poor hut and his ugly, darned breeches, and little by little he began to grow discontented.

He began to wonder why he should be poor and they rich, and he went about his work with such a long face that the birds were afraid of him, and he heaved such deep, grumbling sighs that all the little beasts scuttled into the woods in fright – at least, all save the rabbit.

The rabbit sat back on his haunches, flopped his ears and wobbled his nose. 'Why, what's the matter with you, Rudolf?'

'Nothing,' said Rudolf, grumpily. 'I wish I were rich. That's all.'

'Pah,' said the rabbit. 'What's the good of wishing

without the wishing-skin? Spare your breath, Rudolf.'

Rudolf straightened his back and put down his hatchet. 'Eh?' said he. 'Wishing-skin, did you say? And what may that be, Bunny?'

The rabbit whisked round with a flicker of his white tail. 'Half a minute,' he said, 'I'll show you,' and he skipped behind a bush, returning almost at once with a thin, cobwebby skin. 'There, that's the wishing-skin. But don't tell anyone you've seen it. It belongs to the fairies, and they always hide it. They're afraid of its being stolen. You see it's very valuable. It's made of wishes.'

Rudolf looked at the rabbit out of the corner of his eye, cunningly. 'Bunny,' said he, 'suppose I try it on? I'd like to know what it's like to wear a wishing-skin.'

The rabbit looked doubtful.

'Well,' said he, after a pause, 'I don't know whether I ought to let you do that. It's not mine, and, you know, if you were to wish by accident after you had put it on, the fairies would know and I should get into trouble. You see, whenever you wish, the skin gets a little smaller, because one wish is gone. If you're wearing the wishing-skin all your wishes come true.'

Rudolf's hands began to shake, so he put them behind his back. 'Don't be so silly, Bunny,' said he. 'As if I should get you into trouble. Let me try it on. Come on! See, I've taken off my coat.'

He put his coat on the ground and then – well, then, I'm afraid, he did rather a mean thing. He clapped his hands suddenly so that the rabbit jumped backwards in a fright and before the startled little creature could do anything, Rudolf had put on the wishing-skin and was grinning from ear to ear.

'Ha, ha, ha!' he laughed. 'I wish it would stick to me and become part of me.'

'Oh! Oh!' cried the rabbit. 'Give it back! What will the fairies say? You've made it smaller already.' He stamped with his hind legs on the ground and his eyes looked as if they were going to pop out of his head. 'Do you hear me? Give it back!'

'How can I?' grinned Rudolf. 'It's a part of me, stupid!'

'Oh!' wailed the rabbit. 'Give it back!' And he cried so bitterly that Rudolf was a little ashamed, and somehow, because he was ashamed he grew angry.

'Will you be quiet?' said he. 'I wish you were at the other end of the earth, I do, with your "Give it backs". I –' He stopped and rubbed his eyes. The rabbit had disappeared.

'Why! What?' began Rudolf. Then he remembered. He had wished the rabbit at the other end of the earth, and the wishing-skin had sent it there.

'Hurrah!' shouted Rudolf, capering about. 'Hurrah! Now I can get whatever I want.' And he picked up his coat and ran back to his hut as hard as he could. When he reached the door, he thought for a few minutes, then he walked in and sat down by the fire. 'Wife,' said he, 'have you got a good supper – chicken and sauce and sausages?'

His wife stared at him, half afraid. 'Have you gone mad, Rudolf?' she asked. 'Chicken, sauce, sausages! Here's your good bread and honey.'

'Pooh!' said Rudolf. 'I wish for chicken, sauce and sausages! I wish for wine! I wish for a nice table spread with fine linen, with silver spoons and golden plates! I wish for chairs and velvet cushions!'

'Stop! Stop!' cried his wife, falling into one of the new chairs, for the wishes were coming true every minute. 'How? – What? – Why? –'

'The wishing-skin, my dear,' said her husband. And then he told her all about it.

You should have seen that woman's face. It grew quite red, and the eyes goggled! You ought to have heard what she said. But if you had heard that, well, you wouldn't have heard very much, because she was almost too astonished to speak. But when she recovered from her amazement, she wouldn't give her husband any peace. She simply made him wish all night. It was 'Wish for this!' 'Wish for that!' 'Now wish for fine clothes,' and they found themselves beautifully dressed. 'Now wish for six bags of gold,' and on the table there were six bags of golden coins. 'Now wish for a fine house, and a garden full of flowers and lots and lots of servants.' And instead of the little wooden hut at the edge of the forest, a fine house appeared with a garden full of flowers and servants everywhere! Cooks in the kitchen, butlers in

72

the pantry, maids in the bedrooms, and footmen
with powdered wigs and silk stockings standing on
each side of every stair (and there were three flights
of stairs).

But you know, it was all very well to have such
riches but to tell you the truth, a dreadful thing was
happening! Rudolf's wife was so busy making him
wish, that she didn't notice that her husband was
shrinking. Yes! Rudolf was getting smaller.

You see how it was happening, don't you?

Of course you do! Don't you remember? Rudolf
had wished the skin to become a part of himself.
Each time he wished it became smaller, so of course
he became smaller too.

Poor old Rudolf! He didn't like it at all. He was
afraid to wish himself bigger, because then he might
burst out of the wishing-skin and it would be of no
more use. The difficulty was that his wife wouldn't
be satisfied. She went on making him wish, until at
last she wished that he was a king and she was a
queen in the most beautiful palace in the land.

But, oh dear, it wasn't very nice for Rudolf. You
see, by this time he had become so small that he had
to have his meals, not at the table, but on the table.
He had a special little throne, like a doll's chair, and
a special little table made by the carpenter. They were
put on the big table in the banqueting hall and there
the little king had his meals. This was rather undignified for a king, don't you think? I am afraid everybody who came into the banqueting hall thought

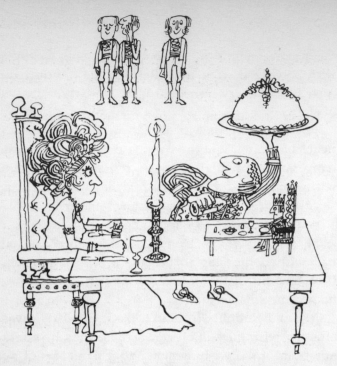

so too, even the servants. They couldn't help being amused when they had to hand the dishes and pour out tiny glasses of wine for the queer little object sitting on the table. And all the grand lords and ladies who came to visit the new king and queen felt exactly the same. They did their best to be polite, but the little king sitting on the table seemed such a joke that they couldn't help playing with him as though he were a toy. And that was dreadful, because Rudolf still had the feelings of a grown-up man, although he was so small.

After a time something happened which was worse still. Rudolf's wife began to despise him. She was offended and angry when people laughed at him because she thought they were laughing at her for having such a silly little husband. She tried to prevent Rudolf from coming into the banqueting hall and hurried him out of the way whenever she was expecting an important visitor. At last, she hid him from sight. She built him a tiny doll's house in the garden and never went to see him except when she wanted him to wish for something.

You can imagine how lonely he was, can't you? Poor little king! He used to get up in the morning and put on his crown and look out of the window, wondering how much smaller he was going to get and whether he would soon disappear altogether.

Then, one day when he was looking out of the window, a woodcutter chanced to walk by. He had a hatchet in his hand and a load of wood on his shoulder, and he walked along the path past the doll's house whistling a tune and looking ever so happy.

Rudolf saw him and sighed deeply, 'Oh!' he cried, 'how I envy that happy man. I wish I could forget all this and be a woodcutter with my wife and cottage again!'

A cold wind suddenly blew in his face. He looked up and – well, if you had peeped into the forest at that moment you would have seen Rudolf picking up a bundle of faggots – and at his feet a little brown rabbit. And the rabbit – yes, I think the rabbit would have been a little out of breath.

The Fox and the Stork

One day a fox thought he would have a bit of a joke at the stork's expense.

He invited him to dinner and served up the soup in very shallow dishes. The fox lapped up his portion very easily but the poor old stork, with his long, thin beak, was quite helpless and unable to manage a single beakful. The fox pretended to be most upset and said he was sorry his guest did not seem to like the soup. The stork did not say anything to this but thanked the fox for his hospitality and left as hungry as when he had arrived.

Shortly after, the stork invited the fox to a return meal. The fox accepted the invitation very readily. However, when the meal was served up he was disgusted to find that the food was in very tall, very narrow dishes, and he hardly managed to get his lips beyond the rim. He had to sit there hungry, watching the stork thrusting his long slender beak right down to the bottom of the dish and gathering up every single morsel of food.

'I am very sorry my food is not to your taste,' said

the stork, pretending to be most concerned.

The fox said nothing but left with a very sour face, muttering to himself, 'It serves me right, I suppose. The stork has certainly paid me back in my own coin.'

Clever Stan and the
Stupid Dragon

Why was Stan Bolovan an unhappy man? He had a comfortable house, two healthy cows and a garden with lots of fruit trees. Well, it was his wife. She was *always* crying. And I mean always. In the morning, after dinner, after supper and even when it was time to go to bed. In other respects she was quite a good sort, really.

You might have thought that she would have told Stan (who was a good husband) *why* she was always crying. But no. She would not tell him. 'Leave me alone,' she would say. 'You wouldn't understand, even if I did tell you.' But he kept on pestering her day after day, week after week, month after month, until at last, one fine day, she *did* tell him. 'I keep crying,' she said tearfully, 'because we haven't got any children.' When Stan heard this, he too became all sad and miserable, and so the Bolovan household wasn't a very cheerful place, I can tell you.

Stan decided to consult a magician. The magician gazed long into the crystal globe and said not a word. Stan waited and waited until at last he became

impatient.

'Come on,' he said, 'I want your help. Say something.'

The magician looked up at him. 'Are you quite certain you want children?' he asked. 'They can be a great burden, you know.'

'Yes, I know,' said Stan, 'but what a happy burden; it's the kind of burden my wife and I are dying to have.'

'Very well then,' said the magician, 'you shall have your wish.'

Stan left with a light heart and started back on his journey home (for he had come a long way to see the magician). He was longing to tell his wife the good news. 'How marvellous!' he thought. 'There'll be no more crying from now on, not from my wife at any rate.'

Imagine his surprise, when he reached the door of his house, at hearing the sound of children's voices laughing and chattering, and little feet pattering all over the place. He went round into the garden and a wonderful sight met his eyes. There were dozens and dozens of children of all shapes and sizes, fat ones and thin ones, tall ones and short ones, children with fair hair and blue eyes and children with dark hair and brown eyes, children with curls and children with straight hair, quiet children and noisy children, cheeky children and shy children – in fact every imaginable variety.

'Good heavens,' said Stan Bolovan to his wife, 'there must be at least a hundred children here!'

'And every one of them welcome,' smiled his wife.

'But how on earth are we going to clothe and feed them all?' asked Stan, perplexed. But his wife only went on smiling. He soon found that she had given all the milk and all the fruit to the children and there wasn't a morsel of food left in the house.

So Stan Bolovan set out to find food and clothing for his children.

After walking for nearly a whole day, he espied a shepherd who was herding his many sheep and lambs in a field.

'I know it's the wrong thing to do,' thought poor Stan Bolovan, 'but if I wait till it's dark I might be able to get a lamb or two and feed my hungry children with some juicy meat.' He hid behind a stout oak tree and waited for night to fall. Suddenly, round about midnight, he heard a great whirring, rushing sound in the skies and lo and behold! he looked up and saw a dragon swooping from a great height straight down among the sheep. It picked up a lamb in each of its four paws and flew up again.

The poor old shepherd was running all over the place, trying to keep his fear-crazed flock together and Stan Bolovan decided to help him. At last, when they had restored some sort of order, they sat down against a tree to rest.

'You know,' sighed the shepherd, 'this happens every single night. If things go on like this I soon won't have a sheep to my name.' He thanked Stan for his help and offered him some bread and cheese. This made Stan feel very much better.

'What will you give me,' he asked, 'if I rid you of that dragon?'

'I'll give you as much food and drink as you like, as well as three rams, three sheep and three lambs.'

'That's a bargain,' said Stan, not having the slightest idea how he was going to conquer the dragon.

He spent the next day helping the shepherd and thinking about his hungry brood of children. As night drew on, a great dread seized him and it was all he could do to stop himself shaking and shivering with fear.

At midnight the air was suddenly filled with the fierce whirring and rushing sound and the fearsome dragon, his scales gleaming in the moonlight, came

81

swooping down amid the sheep.

Stan Bolovan, feeling quite crazily bold, stood up and bawled: 'Stop! Stop at once!'

The beast, quite taken aback, sank slowly to the ground.

'And may I inquire to whom I 'ave the honour of speakin'?' he said somewhat breathlessly.

'I am Stan Bolovan. Stan Bolovan the Mighty, eater-up of rocks and gobbler of mountains. One move from you towards those sheep and I'll gobble *you* up.'

The dragon, for want of anything better to say, muttered grimly: 'You'll have to fight me first.'

'Please don't invite me to fight you,' said Stan Bolovan. 'I'd kill you with one breath and your corpse would be nice filling for my sandwiches.'

The dragon was a terrible coward at heart.

'Well, I've got to be goin' now,' he said. 'I'll bid ye goodnight.'

'Steady on,' said Stan, 'we've got an account to settle first, haven't we now?'

'What? What? What account?' asked the dragon nervously.

'Those sheep you've been stealing every night,' said Stan Bolovan. 'They are my sheep, you know. That man over there is a shepherd who works for me. You'd better settle up here and now, or there'll be trouble.'

The dragon, of course, had no money on him and he had no wish to be made into filling for Stan's sandwiches, so he said: 'My old mother has stacks and stacks of money. Come and stay with us just for three or four days and help her about the house. If she likes you, she'll give you ten sacks of gold every day.'

'Very well,' said Stan Bolovan, getting bolder and bolder every minute. 'Lead me to her.' He thought what a lot of food and clothing ten sacks of gold would buy for his hundred children. 'I'll face the old dragoness even if it kills me.'

So off they went to the dragon's residence and found the dragon's mother waiting outside the door. Her first words were not terribly encouraging. 'What!' she shrieked, her scales standing up in fury. 'No sheep!'

'Sh!' said the dragon soothingly. 'I've brought you a visitor.' And to Stan he whispered: 'Don't worry, I'll go and explain.'

Stan waited outside. He could hear the dragon's quite audible whispers: 'This chap's a terror; he devours rocks and mountains and uses dead dragons as filling for his sandwiches.'

'Leave him to me,' said the mother dragon, not even bothering to lower her voice, 'I'll see to him.'

They called Stan in and showed him to a great bed where he was to sleep for the night. But he hardly had a wink of sleep. He kept having nightmares about the mother dragon with her bulging green eyes and ugly black scales.

Next morning she said to Stan: 'Let me see whether

you are really stronger than my son.' And she picked
up an enormous metal barrel bound round with iron
hoops. The dragon took hold of it and hurled it with
all his might and Stan heard it crash into the ground
at what seemed like miles and miles away. He and
the dragon walked after it and found it buried in the
earth of a mountain-side about three miles off.

'Your turn,' said the dragon. Stan Bolovan, playing for time, looked down at it and sighed.

'Well, what are ye waitin' for?' asked the dragon.

'I'm just thinking,' began Stan slowly. 'What a pity it would be if I had to kill you with this beautiful barrel.'

'What d'ye mean?' asked the dragon.

'Well, just take a look at my hands,' answered Stan, holding out his hands with fingers outspread, as though there was something special about them. 'D'you see those magnetic veins? Anything I throw *always comes back*, and if this barrel should collide with your head in passing, there'd be one nice cracked dragon's skull lying around.'

'Oh,' said the dragon nervously. 'There's no great hurry for you to have your turn just yet. Let's have something to eat first. I'm feeling hungry.' And he went back to his house and brought back great stacks of food and they both sat down and ate their fill, right up till evening when the moon came up.

'Well,' said Stan Bolovan, standing up and stretching himself, 'I suppose I ought to have my throw now, but I'd better wait till the moon goes down in the sky, because if the barrel happens to land on the moon, it's liable to get stuck there for ever. You wouldn't want to lose it, would you?'

'Oh no,' said the dragon hastily. 'It's me mother's favourite barrel. Better not risk throwing it yet. In fact, better not throw it at all, in case it gets stuck on some planet or other.'

'But I must,' protested Stan Bolovan. 'Your mother distinctly said I must. It's a test of strength, remember?'

'I'll tell ye what,' proposed the dragon. 'Let *me* throw it back towards the house. I'll make it go farther this time and I'll tell her that you did it. Then you'll have beaten me, and Mother will never know a thing.'

'No!' replied Stan emphatically. 'No! No! No!'

But when the dragon offered him twenty sacks of gold not to throw the barrel, he said: 'Oh, very well, if you feel so strongly about it . . .'

Then the dragon returned to the house and told his mother that Stan had beaten him once again and had thrown the barrel a good mile further than he had. 'Oh dearie me,' said the mother and she began to feel rather scared.

But by next morning she had another plan to get rid of Stan Bolovan.

'Go and fetch me water from the spring,' she said giving them twenty big buffalo skins. 'Let's see which of you can carry most in one day.'

The dragon started first and went backwards and forwards from his house to the spring and from the spring to the house till he had filled and emptied all twenty skins. He then handed them to Stan.

'Your turn,' he said.

Instead of taking them Stan took a knife out of his pocket, bent down and began scratching the earth near the spring.

86

'What on earth are ye up to now?' asked the dragon suspiciously.

'I want to get at this spring,' replied Stan. 'Then I'll carry the whole lot of water in one go. Seems a terrible waste of time going to and fro with those tiny buffalo skins.'

'N-n-no,' said the dragon nervously. 'You mustn't do that. That spring belongs to the local dragon family. It was originally made by my great-great-great-grandfather. Keep your hands off it, please. I'll carry the skins for you in half the time I did it. Mother will be none the wiser.'

'No,' said Stan firmly, and went on digging.

Finally the dragon had to promise him yet another twenty sacks of gold before he could get him to stop. And so the dragon did all the to-ing and fro-ing with the skins, rushing like mad to get it finished before the day was over, while Stan lay resting on his great bed.

The mother dragon got more and more scared on learning that her son had been beaten yet again, but by the next morning she had thought of another plan.

They were told to go to collect wood in the forest, to see which of them would get more. The dragon immediately began wrenching out great oaks as if they were no bigger than matchsticks and arranged them neatly in rows. But Stan climbed to the top of a tree that had a long creeper trailing round it. With this creeper he tied the top of the tree he was sitting

87

on to the top of the next tree.

'I'm tying all the trees together,' he explained to the dragon. 'Then I'll be able to clear the whole forest at one go.'

'No! Please no!' wailed the dragon, his scales visibly shrinking with fear. 'My great-great-great-great-grandfather planted this forest. Please, please don't.'

'Sorry about that,' said Stan Bolovan, 'but I'm not going to trudge to and fro with a mere half dozen trees at a time.'

So the dragon had to promise yet another twenty sacks of gold before Stan finally said, 'Oh very well, if you insist . . .'

The dragons, mother and son, now decided they had had enough and told Stan they would give him another hundred sacks of gold if he would go away and leave them in peace.

Stan, of course, was only too delighted. But how was he going to carry all those heavy sacks of gold back to his house? That night, as he lay awake in his giant bed thinking how to solve this problem, he heard the voices of the mother dragon and her son.

'We shall be ruined,' the mother was saying, 'we'll have nothing left.'

'Well, what is there we can do about it?' the son asked in a rather weak and helpless tone of voice.

'There's only one thing we can do,' replied the mother. 'You must KILL him this very night.'

'*Me* kill '*im*?' exclaimed the son. 'It's 'im who'll kill

me, more likely.'

'Not if you listen to your mother he won't,' said she. 'Now just wait till he's fast asleep, then go in and bash his head with great-grandfather's club.'

'Aha!' thought Stan Bolovan. 'So that's what they're up to!'

He crept quietly out of bed and went outside to the yard where the pigs' trough was. He filled it with earth and dragged it in on to his bed and covered it with blankets. He himself got under the bed and snored as noisily as he could.

Soon he heard the dragon tiptoe into the room, stop by the bedside and bring down the club with a deafening thwack on to the trough. Stan stopped snoring and let out a long-drawn-out groan, as though he were dying. Shortly afterwards he crept out from under the bed and dragged the trough back to its place in the yard, leaving his bed nice and tidy.

When the dragon and his mother beheld Stan next morning, they could hardly believe their eyes.

'G-g-g-good mornin',' said the dragon. ''Ope you slept well on your last night here.'

'I slept fine,' replied Stan, 'just fine. There was a fly or something that crawled over my nose and tickled me rather, but otherwise I slept just fine. So fine, in fact, that I think I'll stay here another night, if you don't mind. It's not all that often I get the chance to sleep in such a comfy bed.'

Both mother and son looked so distinctly uncomfortable when they heard this that Stan

89

continued: 'Well, if I'm really all that unwelcome, I'll leave today. I don't wish to be a burden . . . but on one condition.'

'Any condition, any condition,' said both dragons hastily in unison. 'You name it.'

'You must carry all the sacks of gold back to my house for me. It'd look a bit undignified for the mighty Stan Bolovan to be seen lugging sacks around.'

The dragon was only too eager to comply. He picked up the sacks in his great claws and flung them on to his enormous back.

'Well, I'll say cheeri-ho,' said Stan to the mother dragon, 'and thanks for everything.'

'Not at all, not at all,' she replied and hurriedly locked the door behind him.

Stan and the dragon began their long journey back home. After a trek lasting many hours, Stan could hear the sound of his children's voices in the distance.

He stopped and turned to the dragon.

'Those are my children playing and shouting. I shouldn't think you'd care to meet them. There's about a hundred of them – all just about as strong as I am, and they can be very rough sometimes. Perhaps you'd . . .' But before he could finish his sentence, the dragon had dropped the sacks and fled in terror. He didn't fancy the thought of meeting a hundred young Stan Bolovans!

Just at that moment Stan's wife came out to greet

him, followed by the enormous brood of laughing, jolly children.

There was enough gold in the sacks to feed and clothe them for the rest of their lives.

Eeyore Loses a Tail and Pooh Finds One

The Old Grey Donkey, Eeyore, stood by himself in a thistly corner of the Forest, his front feet well apart, his head on one side, and thought about things. Sometimes he thought sadly to himself, 'Why?' and sometimes he thought, 'Wherefore?' and sometimes he thought, 'Inasmuch as which?' – and sometimes he didn't quite know what he was thinking about. So when Winnie-the-Pooh came stumping along, Eeyore was very glad to be able to stop thinking for a little, in order to say 'How do you do?' in a gloomy manner to him.

'And how are you?' said Winnie-the-Pooh.

Eeyore shook his head from side to side.

'Not very how,' he said. 'I don't seem to have felt at all how for a long time.'

'Dear, dear,' said Pooh, 'I'm sorry about that. Let's have a look at you.'

So Eeyore stood there, gazing sadly at the ground and Winnie-the-Pooh walked all round him once.

'Why, what's happened to your tail?' he said in surprise.

'What *has* happened to it?' said Eeyore.

'It isn't there!'

'Are you sure?'

'Well, either a tail *is* there or it isn't there. You can't make a mistake about it, and yours *isn't* there!'

'Then what is?'

'Nothing.'

'Let's have a look,' said Eeyore, and he turned slowly round to the place where his tail had been a little while ago, and then, finding that he couldn't catch it up, he turned round the other way, until he came back to where he was at first, and then he put his head down, and looked between his front legs, and at last he said, with a long, sad sigh, 'I believe you're right.'

'Of course I'm right,' said Pooh.

'That Accounts for a Good Deal,' said Eeyore gloomily. 'It Explains Everything. No Wonder.'

'You must have left it somewhere,' said Winnie-the-Pooh.

'Somebody must have taken it,' said Eeyore. 'How Like Them,' he added, after a long silence.

Pooh felt that he ought to say something helpful about it, but didn't quite know what. So he decided to do something helpful instead.

'Eeyore,' he said solemnly, 'I, Winnie-the-Pooh, will find your tail for you.'

'Thank you, Pooh,' answered Eeyore. 'You're a real friend,' said he. 'Not Like Some,' he said.

So Winnie-the-Pooh went off to find Eeyore's tail.

It was a fine spring morning in the Forest as he started out. Little soft clouds played happily in a blue sky, skipping from time to time in front of the sun as if they had come to put it out, and then sliding away suddenly so that the next might have his turn. Through them and between them the sun shone bravely; and a copse which had worn its firs all the year round seemed old and dowdy now beside the new green lace which the beeches had put on so prettily. Through copse and spinney marched Bear; down open slopes of gorse and heather, over rocky beds of streams, up steep banks of sandstone into the heather again; and so at last, tired and hungry, to the Hundred Acre Wood. For it was in the Hundred Acre Wood that Owl lived.

'And if anyone knows anything about anything,' said Bear to himself, 'it's Owl who knows something about something,' he said, 'or my name's not Winnie-the-Pooh,' he said. 'Which it is,' he added. 'So there you are.'

Owl lived at The Chestnuts, an old-world residence of great charm, which was grander than anybody else's or seemed so to Bear, because it had both a knocker *and* a bell-pull. Underneath the knocker there was a notice which said:

PLES RING IF AN RNSER IS REQIRD.

Underneath the bell-pull there was a notice which said:

PLEZ CNOKE IF AN RNSR IS NOT REQID.

These notices had been written by Christopher Robin, who was the only one in the forest who could spell; for Owl, wise though he was in many ways, able to read and write and spell his own name WOL, yet somehow went all to pieces over delicate words like MEASLES and BUTTEREDTOAST.

Winnie-the-Pooh read the two notices very carefully, first from left to right, and afterwards, in case he had missed some of it, from right to left. Then to make quite sure, he knocked and pulled the knocker, and he pulled and knocked the bell-rope, and he called out in a very loud voice, 'Owl! I require an answer! It's Bear speaking.' And the door opened and Owl looked out.

'Hallo, Pooh,' he said. 'How's things?'

'Terrible and Sad,' said Pooh, 'because Eeyore, who is a friend of mine, has lost his tail. And he's Moping about it. So could you very kindly tell me how to find it for him?'

'Well,' said Owl, 'the customary procedure in such cases is as follows.'

'What does Crustimoney Proseedcake mean?' said Pooh. 'For I am a Bear of Very Little Brain, and long words Bother me.'

'It means the Thing to Do.'

'As long as it means that, I don't mind,' said Pooh humbly.

'The thing to do is as follows. First, Issue a Reward. Then –'

'Just a moment,' said Pooh, holding up his paw. '*What* do we do to this – what you were saying? You sneezed just as you were going to tell me.'

'I *didn't* sneeze.'

'Yes, you did, Owl.'

'Excuse me, Pooh, I didn't. You can't sneeze without knowing it.'

'Well, you can't know it without something having been sneezed.'

'What I *said* was, "First *Issue* a Reward".'

'You're doing it again,' said Pooh sadly.

'A Reward!' said Owl very loudly. 'We write a

96

notice to say that we will give a large something to anybody who finds Eeyore's tail.'

'I see, I see,' said Pooh, nodding his head. 'Talking about large somethings,' he went on dreamily, 'I generally have a small something about now – about this time in the morning,' and he looked wistfully at the cupboard in the corner of Owl's parlour; 'just a mouthful of condensed milk or what-not, with perhaps a lick of honey –'

'Well then,' said Owl, 'we write out this notice, and we put it up all over the Forest.'

'A lick of honey,' murmured Bear to himself, 'or – or not, as the case may be.' And he gave a deep sigh, and tried very hard to listen to what Owl was saying.

But Owl went on and on, using longer and longer words, until at last he came back to where he started, and he explained that the person to write out this notice was Christopher Robin.

'It was he who wrote the ones on my front door for me. Did you see them, Pooh?'

For some time now Pooh had been saying 'yes' and 'no' in turn, with his eyes shut, to all that Owl was saying, and having said, 'yes, yes,' last time, he said, 'No, not at all,' now, without really knowing what Owl was talking about.

'Didn't you see them?' said Owl, a little surprised. 'Come and look at them now.'

So they went outside. And Pooh looked at the knocker and the notice below it, and he looked at the bell-rope and the notice below it, and the more he looked at the bell-rope, the more he felt that he had seen something like it, somewhere else, some-time before.

'Handsome bell-rope, isn't it?' said Owl.

Pooh nodded.

'It reminds me of something,' he said, 'but I can't think what. Where did you get it?'

'I just came across it in the Forest. It was hanging over a bush, and I thought at first somebody lived there, so I rang it, and nothing happened, and then I rang it again very loudly, and it came off in my hand, and as nobody seemed to want it, I took it home, and –'

'Owl,' said Pooh solemnly, 'you made a mistake. Somebody did want it.'

'Who?'

'Eeyore. My dear friend Eeyore. He was – he was fond of it.'

'Fond of it?'

'Attached to it,' said Winnie-the-Pooh sadly.

So with these words he unhooked it, and carried it back to Eeyore; and when Christopher Robin had nailed it on in its right place again, Eeyore frisked about the forest, waving his tail so happily that Winnie-the-Pooh came over all funny, and had to hurry home for a little snack of something to sustain him. And, wiping his mouth half an hour afterwards, he sang to himself proudly:

Who found the Tail?
  'I,' said Pooh,
'At a quarter to two
  (Only it was quarter to eleven really),
I found the Tail.'

The Ju-ju Man

In the forest the monkeys lived in the tree-tops and the crocodiles lived in the pools and the snakes slept under thick green leaves. In one part of the forest there was a cave made of rock. In the cave lived a Ju-ju man. He made magic in his cave. He could cast spells on people with his magic. He could make people ill and he could make them well again. He could bring good luck or he could bring bad luck. He could find things that were lost and he could make things disappear.

The black people who lived in huts in the forest were afraid of the Ju-ju man. They were afraid he might make them ill or bring them bad luck. So they gave him presents to make him like them and be kind to them.

Sometimes, outside the cave of the Ju-ju man, there would be a bunch of ripe bananas and a bowl of plums and some fresh fish from the river. The Ju-ju man never said thank you for all these presents. He just ate them up and waited for the people to bring him some more. He was very greedy and the presents did not make him kind.

A little black girl named Lily lived in the forest. The lily flowers that grow in the forest can be dark, almost black, as well as white, so the name fitted her well. When she had nothing special to do, she often hid among the bushes and watched the door of the cave where the Ju-ju man lived. She liked to watch him when he swept out his cave with a broom of stiff leaves. He did this every day, after he had had his breakfast.

First the Ju-ju man put all his belongings outside the cave so that he could sweep in the nooks and corners. He put out his cups and bowls, and blankets and cooking pots, and the queer things he used to make spells. While he swept the cave, Lily could look at all his things. He was very rich. He had more things in his cave than Lily and her father and mother and brothers and sisters had in their hut. He had more things than anyone else in the whole of the forest.

One evening, when Lily was watching from among the bushes, a yellow lion cub padded past the cave. The Ju-ju man came to the door and said kindly:

'Good evening, yellow lion cub. Will you come in and have some supper with me? I have plenty for the two of us.'

'Thank you,' said the lion cub and he went into the cave.

Lily waited and waited and waited, but the lion cub never came out again.

101

The next time the Ju-ju man swept out his cave, Lily saw that he had something new. It was a yellow jug. She wondered where it had come from. She had never seen a jug like it in the forest.

One evening, when Lily was watching, a striped tiger strolled past the cave. The Ju-ju man came to the door and said kindly:

'Good evening, striped tiger. Will you come in and have some supper with me? I have plenty for the two of us.'

'Thank you,' said the tiger and he went into the cave.

Lily waited and waited and waited, but the tiger never came out again.

The next time the Ju-ju man swept out his cave, Lily saw that he had something else new. It was a striped mat for the floor. She wondered where it had come from. She had never before seen a mat like it in the forest.

One evening, a grey monkey with a long tail frisked past the cave. The Ju-ju man came to the door and said kindly:

'Good evening, grey monkey. Will you come in and have some supper with me? I have plenty for the two of us.'

'Thank you,' said the grey monkey and he went into the cave.

Lily waited and waited and waited, but the monkey never came out again.

The next time the Ju-ju man swept the cave, Lily

102

saw that he had something else new. It was a grey fur hat with a long tassel. He wore it on his head while he swept and the tassel swung to and fro. She wondered where it had come from. She had never before seen a hat like it in the forest.

One evening, a pink parrot flew by the cave. The Ju-ju man came to the door and said kindly:

'Good evening, pink parrot. Will you come in and have some supper with me? I have plenty for the two of us.'

'Thank you,' said the pink parrot and he went into the cave.

Lily waited and waited and waited, but the parrot never came out again.

The next time the Ju-ju man swept out his cave, Lily saw that he had something else new. It was a fan made of pink feathers. This time she did not wonder who had given it to him. She guessed what had happened. She knew he had cast a spell on the parrot and turned him into a fan.

She also guessed what had happened to the yellow lion cub and the striped tiger and the grey monkey. They had been turned into the yellow jug and the striped mat and the hat with a long tassel.

Lily made up her mind to be very careful and not to let the wicked Ju-ju man turn her into anything by his magic. But one day when she was hiding near the cave, she saw that the Ju-ju man was asleep. His eyes were shut and he was lying quite, quite still. She came out of her hiding place and tickled the sole of his foot with a blade of grass. He did not move. So she was sure he was asleep and not pretending. She crept into his cave on tiptoe to have a good look round.

Lily wanted to see the magic things he used when he put spells on people and turned them into jugs and mats and hats and fans. She saw a bone in a corner. Perhaps it was a magic bone. She was just going to touch it when the Ju-ju man sat up and grabbed her with his skinny black hands.

'Little black girl,' he said kindly, 'will you have supper with me? I have plenty for the two of us.'

'No, thank you,' said Lily. 'I have had my supper.'

'Never mind about that!' said the Ju-ju man. 'You can stay here with me and have some more of my supper. You must. Or I shall have to make you.'

'Very well,' said Lily, who knew she could not get away from the Ju-ju man, he was too strong and cunning.

The Ju-ju man began to stir the broth which was cooking on the fire. While he stirred, Lily looked round the cave.

'You have some nice things in your cave,' said Lily. 'I think you must have everything you need.'

'I have almost all I need,' said the Ju-ju man. 'There's just one thing I want. That is a stool to sit on while I stir my broth.'

'What kind of a stool?' asked Lily.

'A little black stool,' said the Ju-ju man.

Then Lily knew that she must be very careful

104

indeed because the Ju-ju man was going to turn her into a black stool. So she watched everything he did very closely.

When the broth was cooked, he put some into two bowls. And when he thought Lily was not looking, he put a pinch of powder into one bowl and whispered some magic words. He gave this bowl to Lily, and kept the other for himself. But when he was fetching two spoons, and his back was turned, Lily changed the bowls round. She gave him the one with the powder in it.

'Eat up your broth! Eat it up like a good girl!' said the Ju-ju man, rubbing his skinny hands together.

'It is too hot,' said Lily.

'Then blow on it,' said the Ju-ju man.

So Lily blew on her broth to cool it.

'Now eat it up! Spoon it up!' said the Ju-ju man, dancing up and down.

'I don't know how to use a spoon,' said Lily. 'Please show me. We haven't any spoons in our hut.'

'Watch me,' said the Ju-ju man. 'Hold the handle like this. Dip the other end in like this. Lift it up. And drink.' He drank a spoonful to show her.

'Show me again,' begged Lily, and the Ju-ju man drank another spoonful, and she tried to copy him. But her hand was shaking so much that she spilt the broth on the floor.

'Hurry up! Hurry up!' said the Ju-ju man. 'Let's have a race to see who can finish first.' Lily ate as fast as she could, but her hand was still shaking and the Ju-ju man was winning easily.

But when the Ju-ju man had eaten half his broth, he began to shrink and shrink. He grew smaller and smaller. His head got flatter and flatter. His legs got shorter and shorter. Soon he had turned into a little black stool.

Then Lily looked round the cave and found a pot of the magic powder that the Ju-ju man had sprinkled on the soup. She put a pinch on the jug and the mat and the hat and the fan, and they turned back into the lion cub and the tiger and the monkey and the parrot.

Then they all danced for joy and ran home to their mothers. And though the Ju-ju man was now only a black stool, and quite safe, they never went near his cave again.

THE JU-JU MAN

A pinch of his powder,
  A sip of his tea,
And you'll be in his power,
  And never get free.

He'll turn you to something
  He needs for his hut,
It might be an ear-ring,
  A flower or a nut.

So if he should beckon
  And ask you inside,
Run away in the forest!
  Find somewhere to hide!

The Sparrows' Tug-of-War

One summer morning Mother Sparrow was sitting on her nest full of eggs, enjoying the bright summer sunshine. She could hear the other birds chirping merrily away among the trees and the monkeys chattering for all their worth. In fact everything would have been perfect but for one thing – Father Sparrow was cross, very cross.

'It's that ugly old crocodile,' he grumbled. 'I went down to bathe in that nice shallow part of the river, you know, and there he was, spread out all over the place. No room for me at all! And when I very politely told him off, he opened his big mouth and laughed. And do you know what he said? "Go away," he said, "I shall stay here as long as I please. Go and have your dip somewhere else." '

Just as Father Sparrow was speaking, there was a sudden tremendous bump against the tree which tipped him off his twig and very nearly flung Mother Sparrow out of her nest. Father Sparrow flew up to see who it was. It was none other than Brother Elephant taking his morning constitutional. 'Hey there, Brother Elephant,' called out Father Sparrow with a furious chirrup, 'D'you realize that you've nearly shaken my missus out of her nest?'

'Well, what of that, there's no harm done,' answered Brother Elephant, without even apologizing.

'No harm done indeed! You've given her the shock of her life. I warn you, Brother Elephant, if you ever do that again, *I'll tie you up!*'

Brother Elephant gave a mighty guffaw. 'Ho! Ho! Ho! Tie me up indeed! Go ahead, Father Sparrow. You and all the other sparrows. You are perfectly welcome to tie me up. *But you won't keep me tied.* Neither you nor all the sparrows in the whole wide world.' And off he stamped, still guffawing.

'We'll see about that,' twittered Father Sparrow, his feathers all a-fluff. Still furiously angry, he flew down to the river where he found the crocodile still all a-sprawl, sunning himself in the nice shallow part of the river.

'I give you warning, Crocodile,' chirped Father Sparrow sternly (whereupon the crocodile lazily opened one eye), 'that if you are not out of this place by tomorrow morning, *I shall tie you up.*'

'Tie me up as much as you like,' answered the crocodile closing his eye, 'and welcome to it. *But you can't keep me tied* – neither you nor all the sparrows in the whole wide world.'

'We'll see about that,' said Father Sparrow and whisking his tail he flew back to Mother Sparrow.

All the rest of the day he was very busy discussing

109

matters with all the other sparrows in the forest. And in the afternoon, several hundreds of them got together and, working very hard, they finally made a long length of creeper, very thick and very stout – as strong as any rope.

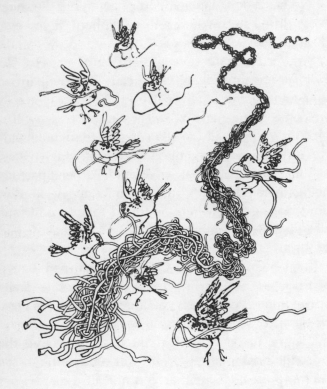

Soon Brother Elephant came crashing through the forest and, Doying! came bump against Father Sparrow's tree.

'And now what are you going to do, Father

110

Sparrow?' asked Brother Elephant. 'Ready to tie me up, eh?'

'Yes, we are,' replied Father Sparrow. And he and all his friends flew up and round and round and down and up again with the long creeper-rope between their beaks, till it was all tightly bound round Brother Elephant's enormous body.

'Now listen to me, Brother Elephant,' said Father Sparrow, 'when I give the word "PULL", pull as hard as you can.'

'Rightee-ho,' answered Brother Elephant, guffawing and shaking with laughter.

But all the sparrows had flown away with the other end of the creeper-rope, pulling it through bush and tree, till they came to the river where Crocodile was.

'So you've come to tie me up, Father Sparrow?' he asked, opening a lazy eye.

'Yes, that's exactly what we *are* going to do,' came the reply.

'Tie away,' said Crocodile and the sparrows set to work pecking and tugging, flying up and down and up and down again and again and round and round, till the rope was tight and firm round Crocodile's long, slimy body.

'Now,' said Father Sparrow, 'when I say "PULL", don't forget, *pull*.'

'Right,' said Crocodile, half asleep, and the sparrows whisked their tails and flew off.

Then Father Sparrow perched himself in the middle of the creeper-rope where neither Brother

111

Elephant nor Crocodile could see him (and neither of *them* could see the other), and then, IN A VERY LOUD CHIRP, he called 'PULL'.

You can well imagine Crocodile's surprise when he found himself jerked out of his sleep and half-way up the river bank. You can also imagine Brother Elephant's astonishment when, a couple of seconds later, *he* found himself pulled off his feet – by Crocodile tugging back. Of course, they both thought it was Father Sparrow who was pulling them.

'What a mighty sparrow!' thought Brother Elephant.

'That little bird certainly knows how to pull!' thought Crocodile.

And so now the tug-of-war began in earnest. They each pulled with all their might and main. Sometimes Brother Elephant would gain the upper hand for a few minutes and Crocodile would be dragged up the river bank. Sometimes Crocodile would pull more strongly and Brother Elephant would have to dig his big feet into the earth to stop himself being pulled over. The contest was pretty even, and it went on and on with both of them puffing and panting and groaning, and all the sparrows watching from up above twittered and laughed and enjoyed themselves hugely.

Towards evening, when the sun was beginning to set, Crocodile said to himself, 'I'd better not let the other animals see me in this state when they come down to drink at the river.' So he called out: 'Oh, please, Father Sparrow, please stop tugging and untie me. I promise never to take your bathing place again.'

And Brother Elephant cried out in a tiny trumpet: 'Father Sparrow, if you stop pulling and untie me, I promise I will never bump into your tree again.'

'Oh, very well,' said Father Sparrow, 'very well.'

And so all the sparrows set to work again, hopping and pulling and pecking and chattering, until they had untied Crocodile, who then slid, shamefaced, into the river among the tall reeds and hid himself until it was pitch dark. Then they went and did the same thing to Brother Elephant who then trod quietly away (almost on tip-toe!), thoroughly ashamed of being beaten by such a tiny bird. And all the sparrows, satisfied with their day's work, whisked their tails and flew away.

And Father Sparrow was now able to live in peace and take his dip in his favourite shallow part of the river. And Mother Sparrow was able to sit quietly on her nest of eggs.

The Brave Little Tailor

There was a lovely plate of white bread and jam on the little table next to the tailor as he sat sewing on that very hot summer day. But the trouble was it was *so* hot that lots of horrible flies kept buzzing round and landing on the bread and jam.

'Confound them!' cried the little tailor, and he got so impatient that he lifted his damp ironing-cloth and brought it down with a great swish on top of them. When he took the cloth away, there were seven dead flies scattered on the table and plate.

'Aha!' cried the little tailor triumphantly. 'Seven at one blow! What a hero I am!' And he straightway set to work to make himself a belt, and on it he wrote the words: SEVEN AT ONE BLOW.

As he gazed at these brave words, written in very large letters, the tailor felt very proud of himself.

'Seven at one blow,' he thought to himself. 'I must go out into the world and show what a great hero I am. I cannot spend the rest of my days in this tiny town.' So he set out the next morning with a chunk of cheese in his pocket and his pet bird on his wrist, whistling a merry tune as he walked gaily along.

Very soon he met a huge giant who was taller than any of the houses along the street.

'Would you care to accompany me on my travels?' the tailor called out to him. 'Just look at this,' he continued, pointing to his belt. 'Seven at one blow – that's what I've done. That's how strong I am.'

The huge giant looked down at the little tailor with tremendous scorn.

'Strong!' he bawled. 'Strong! D'you call that strong! We'll soon see how strong you are.' And he picked up a large stone and squeezed it till water dripped from it. 'Can you do that?' he asked. 'Can you do that, little man?'

'That's nothing,' said the little tailor airily and he took the hunk of cheese out of his pocket and squeezed it till the whey oozed freely from it.

The giant grunted. He looked round for another large stone, picked it up and threw it up high into the clouds.

'Let's just see whether you can do that,' he said.

'I notice that your stone came back down again, even though it went up into the clouds,' remarked the little tailor. 'When I throw mine up, you'll never see it again.' And he threw his little pet bird up into the sky. Of course, the little creature was so glad to find itself soaring high in the sky that it flew far away, never to return.

The giant grunted even more at this. He pointed to a huge tree that had fallen across the way and said, 'Let's see how hard you can work without getting tired. Just carry this tree with me.'

'Right,' said the little tailor briskly. 'I'd better take the heavier end where all the thick branches are,' and he very nimbly slipped among the leaves where he was completely hidden from view, so that the giant carried both tree and tailor without knowing it. The giant strode along for a while with his enormous burden but he soon got tired and dropped the tree to the ground with a tremendous groan.

The little tailor jumped noislessly out.

'Tired already?' he asked. 'I'm as fresh as a daisy!' And whistling gaily the little tailor walked briskly beside the giant, who was still groaning.

They kept going for some time, the little tailor humming and whistling cheerfully all the time and the giant looking more and more worried. Suddenly his huge face lit up.

'D'you see that apple tree over there?' he asked. 'Come and help yourself to a few rosy ones.' And so saying he stretched out his long arm, pulled down a branch and called, 'Catch!' The little tailor was taken by surprise. He couldn't hold the branch down, of course, and when the giant let go he was flung high up into the air and came down again with a mighty bump.

'So you couldn't manage to hold that tiny twig?' said the giant. 'You are a weakling, aren't you?'

The little tailor had recovered his wits.

'I was merely jumping over the top of the tree – to

116

avoid that man with the gun, over there. He was
about to fire and I got out of his way just in time.'
He said all this very coolly.

This made the giant angrier than ever. 'I'll get even
with this little dwarf yet,' he muttered to himself.

117

'Would you like to spend the night in my cave?' he called down. The tailor accepted very politely and they were soon inside a deep, dark cave where there were ten giants eating whole sheep with their fingers. The giant pointed to a bed big enough for fifty tailors and wished him goodnight. When he was alone, the tailor took the pillow off the bed and lay down on it. Even the pillow was very much bigger than an ordinary bed and gave the tailor ample room.

In the dead of night the giant came in and gave the bed a mighty whack with a stout stick. 'Well, that's the end of that little boaster,' he muttered. 'Seven at one blow, indeed!' Then he went back to bed. But as soon as he had gone, the little tailor crept out of his pillow-bed and set off on his travels again, as cheerful as ever. He had not gone far when he met seven smart Soldiers of the King. One of them saw the words SEVEN AT ONE BLOW on the tailor's belt and he called them all to a halt.

'Hey you,' he called out, 'you'll be mighty useful to our King if you can fight as well as you claim. Come along with us.' And so the little tailor marched along with the seven smart Soldiers of the King.

The King was indeed delighted with this doughty new recruit and he said to the tailor: 'There are two monster giants killing and robbing my people. If you can get rid of them, you shall marry the Princess, my daughter, and have half my kingdom.'

'That will be well within my powers, Your Majesty,' replied the little tailor and he immediately

118

set off in search of the two giants. He found them asleep under a tree in the forest. They were snoring so powerfully that the trees shook, as though in a storm, every time they breathed. The tailor filled a bag of stones and climbed up into a tree. He threw a stone at one of the giants and caught him beautifully right on the tip of his nose. He awoke in a fury and roared at the other one: 'How dare you bang me on the nose!'

'I don't know what on earth you are talking about,' replied the other. 'I did nothing of the kind.' They quarrelled and argued violently for quite some time but finally went off to sleep again. This time the little tailor threw a stone and hit the second giant on the nose. He jumped up in a great rage and roared, 'So you are having your revenge after all, are you?' They both got on their feet and began fighting each other hammer and tongs. They wrenched huge trees out of the ground to use as weapons and the end of it was that they killed each other.

The little tailor then got down from the tree and went back to the King to claim his reward.

'Not just yet, brave little tailor,' replied His Majesty. 'There is one more task I must ask you to perform. There is a unicorn running wild in the forest and I want you to bring it back alive to me.'

'Only one, Your Majesty?' said the little tailor coolly. 'I'll catch seven if you like.'

So off he went back to the forest, but this time he took with him a long coil of rope and an axe. He espied

119

the unicorn from afar; it was making straight for him with its horn sticking out of its forehead like a spear.

The tailor stood firm in its path until the very last second and then skipped aside so that the unicorn careered on and got its horn stuck deep in the trunk of a tree. The tailor wound the rope round its neck and chopped away the part of the trunk where the beast had its horn stuck fast. Then he marched it in triumph back to the palace.

The King was pleased but he still would not give the tailor his just reward.

'There's one last thing you must do,' said the King. 'You must catch the wild boar that is killing my woodcutters.'

'Only one?' asked the little tailor airily, and off he went once more, humming and whistling, and refusing the offer of help from the King's huntsmen. But when he saw the terrible boar with its savage tusks, he had a bit of a fright and ran away as fast as he could until he came to a little chapel where the door was open. In he rushed, with the boar thundering after him. But the little tailor, recovering his wits, sprang through a tiny window and then came back round and firmly locked the chapel door. The boar was now a prisoner and the tailor went back to tell the King of his capture.

This time the King could not refuse his reward, so the little tailor who had killed SEVEN AT ONE BLOW married the Princess and in due time became King himself.

120

The Tiger, the Brahmin and the Jackal

The people of a tiny village in India were very angry with a certain tiger who used to come marauding among their poor homes every evening. One night several of their brave men went out with a large net, caught him and locked him fast in a cage, where they left him snarling his lungs out.

One day a Brahmin happened to be walking along close by and he heard the terrible noise. When he got near the cage, the Tiger cried out, 'Oh brother Brahmin, brother Brahmin! have pity on me. Please unlock this cage so that I may go and quench my thirst in the stream.'

The Brahmin was terrified. 'Brother Tiger,' he said, 'if I let you out will you not eat me?'

'Oh, indeed to goodness no, I will not,' replied the Tiger. 'How could I possibly be so ungrateful to one who has saved my life? All I want is a little drink of water.'

So the Brahmin opened the door of the cage. But no sooner was the Tiger outside than he said, 'Now I am going to eat you. And then I shall have a

refreshing drink.'

'Oh, Brother Tiger,' pleaded the Brahmin, quivering with terror, 'what about your promise? And, besides, is it right that you should eat me when I have just set you free?'

'It is both right and fair,' replied the Tiger. 'I am now going to eat you.'

'*Please* do not act in haste,' implored the Brahmin. 'Let us first seek the opinions of five of our brothers and if they all agree that it is right and fair that you should eat me, then I am willing to die.'

'Very well,' said the Tiger, 'so be it.'

So the Brahmin and the Tiger walked along together till they came to a Banyan Tree.

'Brother Banyan,' said the Brahmin, 'is it right and fair that Brother Tiger should eat me after I have set him free from his cage?'

The Banyan Tree replied in a slow, gloomy tone: 'When the sun is hot in high summer, men come and rest in the cool of my shady branches. But in the evening, when they are no longer hot and weary, they get up and break my twigs and scatter my leaves. They show no gratitude. I say, let the Tiger eat the Brahmin.'

The Tiger was pleased with this but the Brahmin said: 'That is only one opinion. We have yet to ask another four.'

So they walked on for a while until they met a camel.

'Brother Camel,' said the Brahmin, 'do you find it

123

right and fair that Brother Tiger should eat me when I set him free from his cage?'

The Camel replied in lazy tones: 'In my young days when I worked with all the vigour of my youthful body, my master took good care of me and fed me well. But now when I am old he makes me work harder than ever before, places heavy burdens on my back and beats me when I am weary. There is no justice among men. I say, let the Tiger eat the Brahmin.'

The Tiger was about to pounce upon the Brahmin, but the latter reminded him that there were still three opinions to be heard, and so they continued to walk until, after a while, they saw an eagle flying above their heads.

The Brahmin called to him, 'Brother Eagle, Brother Eagle! Does it seem right and fair to you that Brother Tiger should eat me when I have just let him free from his cage?'

The Eagle paused in his flight and soared low above them.

'I am a bird of the skies,' he replied, 'and do no harm to any man. Yet men come and rob my nest and shoot at me with their murderous weapons. Men are cruel creatures. Therefore I say, let the Tiger eat the Brahmin.'

The Tiger was more ready than ever to spring upon the Brahmin but the Brahmin again reminded him that there were still two opinions to be heard.

So on they walked until by and by they came to a

124

river bank where an alligator was basking in the sun.

'Oh, Brother Alligator,' implored the Brahmin. 'Tell us whether you judge that it is right and fair that Brother Tiger should eat me in return for my kindness in setting him free from captivity.'

The Alligator replied without even turning his head: 'When men approach the river bank I have to hide in the water, for they are for ever trying to catch me and kill me. They give me no peace. My judgement is, let the Tiger eat the Brahmin.'

The Tiger purred with glee but the Brahmin still had hope and told the Tiger to have patience until they had heard the fifth and final opinion.

After walking some distance further they came upon a jackal.

'Brother Jackal, oh, Brother Jackal,' cried the Brahmin in his most imploring voice. 'Is it right and fair that Brother Tiger should eat me when I have given him his freedom?'

The Jackal looked puzzled. 'Pray tell me what this is all about,' he said.

'I found Brother Tiger locked up in a cage,' the Brahmin explained, 'and he asked me to let him out so that he could quench his thirst in a nearby stream. But no sooner was he out of the cage than he wanted to eat me.'

'What kind of cage was it?' asked the Jackal.

'A large, iron cage,' replied the Brahmin.

'And you let him out of this large, iron cage?'

'Yes, Brother Jackal,' answered the Brahmin.

'I really do not understand. I do not understand this at all,' said the Jackal. 'You will have to take me to the spot where this cage is, so that I may see it for myself.'

So the Tiger, the Brahmin and the Jackal all walked back to the place where the large, iron cage stood.

'Now, let me see,' said the Jackal, walking slowly round the cage and examining it very carefully. 'Where were you exactly at the beginning of this whole affair?'

'I was simply here on the roadside wending my way along,' replied the Brahmin.

'And you, Tiger, where were you?' asked the Jackal.

'I was inside the cage,' replied the Tiger.

'Please bear with me a little longer,' continued the Jackal. 'I still have not got a clear picture of the situation. Would you be so very kind as to show me where exactly you were in the cage. In the front of the cage, perhaps, or at the back, or just prowling around in the middle.'

'If you *must* know,' said the Tiger with some show of impatience, 'I was standing just here, on this precise spot,' and he walked into the cage to show the Jackal exactly where he had been when the Brahmin was passing.

'Oh, thank you, Tiger, that makes the matter much clearer,' said the Jackal. 'But forgive me if I press for a few more details. I still fail to understand why you did not come out of the cage by yourself.'

126

'The door was shut,' replied the Tiger briefly.

'Oh yes, of course, of course,' mused the Jackal. 'By the way, how does this cage-door shut?'

'It shuts like this,' said the Brahmin, pushing the door to.

'And does this particular door lock?' inquired the Jackal. 'And if it does, does it lock from the outside or from the inside?'

'It locks like this,' said the Brahmin. And he bolted the door of the cage.

Then the Jackal said, 'Now that the door is shut and bolted, Brother Brahmin, I think it advisable to leave it so.' And he cried out to the Tiger. 'You, Tiger, are a wicked and ungrateful creature. When the kind Brahmin let you out to quench your thirst, you were ready to eat him in return for his good deed. I hope no one will ever set you free again.'

And to the Brahmin the Jackal said: 'Farewell, Brother Brahmin. Go on your way in peace.' And he ran off, leaving the Brahmin a happy and grateful man.

Mr Miacca

Tommy Grimes was sometimes a good boy, and sometimes a bad boy; and when he was a bad boy, he was a very bad boy. Now his mother used to say to him: 'Tommy, Tommy, be a good boy, and don't go out of the street, or else Mr Miacca will take you.' But still when he was a bad boy he would go out of the street; and one day, sure enough, he had scarcely got round the corner, when Mr Miacca did catch him and popped him into a bag upside down, and took him off to his house.

When Mr Miacca got Tommy inside, he pulled him out of the bag and sat him down, and felt his arms and legs. 'You're rather tough,' says he; 'but you're all I've got for supper, and you'll not taste bad boiled. But body o' me, I've forgot the herbs, and it's bitter you'll taste without herbs. Sally! Here, I say, Sally!' and he called Mrs Miacca.

So Mrs Miacca came out of another room and said: 'What d'ye want, my dear?'

'Oh, here's a little boy for supper,' said Mr Miacca, 'and I've forgot the herbs. Mind him, will ye, while

128

I go for them.'

'All right, my love,' says Mrs Miacca, and off he goes.

Then Tommy Grimes said to Mrs Miacca: 'Does Mr Miacca always have little boys for supper?'

'Mostly, my dear,' said Mrs Miacca, 'if little boys are bad enough, and get in his way.'

'And don't you have anything else but boy-meat? No pudding?' asked Tommy.

'Ah, I loves pudding,' says Mrs Miacca. 'But it's not often the likes of me gets pudding.'

'Why, my mother is making a pudding this very day,' said Tommy Grimes, 'and I'm sure she'd give you some, if I ask her. Shall I run and get some?'

'Now that's a thoughtful boy,' said Mrs Miacca, 'only don't be long and be sure to be back for supper.'

So off Tommy pelted, and right glad he was to get off so cheap; and for many a long day he was as good as good could be, and never went round the corner of the street. But he couldn't always be good; and one day he went round the corner, and as luck would have it, he hadn't scarcely got round it when Mr Miacca grabbed him up, popped him in his bag, and took him home.

When he got him there, Mr Miacca dropped him out; and when he saw him, he said: 'Ah, you're the youngster that served me and my missus such a shabby trick, leaving us without any supper. Well, you shan't do it again. I'll watch over you myself. Here, get under the sofa, and I'll sit on it and watch the pot boil for you.'

So poor Tommy Grimes had to creep under the sofa, and Mr Miacca sat on it and waited for the pot to boil. And they waited and they waited, but still the pot didn't boil, till at last Mr Miacca got tired of waiting, and he said: 'Here, you under there, I'm not going to wait any longer; put out your leg, and I'll stop you giving us the slip.'

So Tommy put out a leg and Mr Miacca got a chopper, and chopped it off, and pops it in the pot.

Suddenly he calls out: 'Sally, my dear, Sally!' and nobody answered. So he went into the next room to look for Mrs Miacca, and while he was there Tommy crept out from under the sofa and ran out of the door. For it was a leg of the sofa that he had put out.

So Tommy Grimes ran home, and he never went round the corner again till he was old enough to go alone.

The Chatterbox

Once upon a time there lived a young man and his young wife, Tatiana. The wife was a terrible gossip, and she couldn't keep a thing to herself. As soon as she heard a piece of news the whole village knew about it at once.

One day the man went to the forest and began to dig out a wolves' lair, and there he found a treasure. He thought to himself: 'Now what shall I do? As soon as my wife knows about this, the whole district will ring with the news: they'll hear about it in every house for miles. It will get to our master's ears and then I can say goodbye to the treasure – it'll have to go to him.'

He thought for a long time and finally he hit upon a plan. He buried the treasure in the earth, took careful note of the spot, and started off for home. When he came to the river, he examined the fishnet he had set there the day before and found a fine perch caught in it. He pulled it out and went on his way. Then he came to the trap he had set in the forest and there was a hare caught in it. He loosed the hare and put the perch in the trap; and he took the hare back to the river and pushed it into the net.

When he got home, he said to his wife:

'Well, Tatiana, heat the oven and bake as many pancakes as you can.'

'Have you gone mad?' said his wife. 'Whoever heard of heating the oven at night? And who'll want to eat pancakes so late?'

'Don't argue, just do as you're told,' said the man. 'I've found a treasure in the forest and we must bring it home after dark.'

At this good news, Tatiana began to warm the oven and bake the pancakes.

'Eat, dearest husband, eat them while they're hot.'

The man ate one pancake and slipped two or three into his sack. Then he ate another one and did the same thing again; his wife didn't notice what he was doing.

'You seem to be very hungry today! I can't make the pancakes fast enough,' she said to him.

'Well, it's a long way to go and the treasure is heavy, so I must eat my fill.'

When he had filled up his sack with pancakes he said, 'I've had enough. Now have some yourself, but hurry, for we must be on our way.' So she ate as many pancakes as she wanted, and then they set out together.

The night was dark. The man walked on a little ahead of his wife, and as he went he hung the pancakes he had slipped into his sack on to the

133

branches of the trees.

His wife saw the pancakes on the trees.

'Look, look,' she cried, 'there are pancakes growing on the trees!'

'Why not? There's nothing odd in that! Didn't you see the pancake cloud that passed a minute ago?'

'No, I saw nothing, I was too busy watching my feet and finding my way among the roots.'

'Come along,' called the man, 'there's a trap here for a hare; let's have a look at it.'

They got to the trap and the man pulled out the perch.

'Oh, husband dear, how could a fish get into a snare?'

'Did you not know that there are perches that can walk?' he said.

'Indeed I didn't!' said Tatiana. 'Had I not seen it with my own eyes, I wouldn't have believed it!'

They came to the river and Tatiana said:

'Your net is here somewhere. I wonder if there are any fish in it?'

'We may as well look,' said he.

So they dragged out the net and there they found the hare. Tatiana raised her hands to heaven.

'Oh, Lord!' she cried. 'What's the world coming to? A hare in a net!'

'You silly young thing, what's so surprising in that? Haven't you ever seen a water-hare?'

'That's just the point,' she said, 'I haven't.'

By this time they had come to the spot where he

had buried the treasure. The man dug it up and filled his and his wife's sacks with gold, and they turned back towards home. Their path ran near the master's house. As they came near the house they heard the bleating of sheep.

'Oh, how dreadful!' said Tatiana, who by now was frightened of her own shadow. 'What is it?'

Her husband replied:

'Run! Run for your life! It's the fiends of hell tormenting our master! Don't let them see us!'

They ran home, panting. The man hid the gold, and they went to sleep.

'Now be careful, Tatiana, not a word to anyone about the treasure or harm will come to us.'

'Of course, dear husband,' she replied. 'Be sure I will say nothing.'

Next day they got up late. The wife lit a good fire and when the blue smoke began to curl up the chimney she took her pails and went to fetch some water. At the well the other women were also getting water and said to her:

'Your stove is lit very late today, Tatiana.'

'Oh, my dears,' she said, 'I've been up all night; that's why I slept late.'

'What were you doing at night then?'

'My husband found a treasure and we went to fetch the gold after dark.'

That day the whole village rang with the tale of how Tatiana and her husband had found a treasure and carried home two sacks of gold.

Towards dusk the news reached the ears of their master. He ordered Tatiana's husband to his house.

'How dare you hide from me this treasure you found on my land?' he said.

'I know nothing of any treasure,' replied the man.

'Don't lie to me!' cried the master. 'I know everything. It's your own wife who has spread the news.'

'But, Honourable Master, she's not right in the head!' Tatiana's husband said. 'She imagines things!'

'We'll soon see about that!'

And the master summoned Tatiana.

'Did your husband find a treasure?'

'Yes, he did, sir, indeed he did.'

'And did you both go at night to fetch the gold?'

'We did, sir, yes we did.'

'Tell me all that happened.'

'First we went through the forest, and there were pancakes hanging on the trees. . . .'

136

'Pancakes on the trees?'

'Why, yes, out of the pancake cloud! Then we saw the hare's trap and found a perch in it. We took the perch and went on towards the river and there we pulled out the net – and lo and behold it had caught a hare! We let him go. Not far from the river was the treasure. We filled our sacks with gold and went home. And just at that time, as we were passing near your house, we heard the fiends of hell tormenting your lordship.'

At this point the master could bear it no longer, and he stamped his foot.

'Get out of my sight, you stupid woman!'

'You see,' said the man, 'you really can't believe a word she says.'

'Yes, I see that very well. You can go.'

They went home and the two of them had enough to live on ever after, so clever had the young man been with his gossiping wife.

Axe Soup

Once upon a long time ago there was a handsome young soldier. He had fought in the wars for many a long year and was now on his way home. He was feeling tired and hungry and was just about to lie down in the woods to rest his weary legs when he espied a wooden house in the distance. He dragged himself up to the door and knoccked. There was no reply, so he knocked again. There was still no reply, so he turned the knob and pushed the door open. It all looked so cosy and comfortable inside and there was such a delicious smell of food that he felt very tempted to walk in and help himself. Just then a little old woman appeared.

'Good-day to you,' said the soldier. 'Excuse me for arriving so unexpectedly. I did knock but there was no answer. I am so hungry, I could eat an ox. I haven't touched a morsel of food for two days.'

The old woman looked at the soldier but said not a word.

'Could you perhaps offer me just a little soup?' asked the soldier, 'and then I'll be on my way again.'

After a very long pause the woman said slowly, 'I am very poor, I have no food in the house to offer you.'

The young soldier was not only handsome. He was clever too. He could smell the food, so he knew the old woman was not telling the truth.

'I'll tell you what,' he said, 'I could make you a really delicious soup out of my old axe here.' And he pointed to the rather rusty thing slung over his shoulder. 'You just find me a saucepan and fill it with water and I'll do the rest.'

The old woman went and brought him what he asked for. The soldier placed the saucepan on the fire and then just sat and waited. The old woman also sat down and watched him with great curiosity.

After a while the soldier carefully put his axe into the saucepan, sat down and waited again. A few minutes later he put a spoon in the saucepan and tasted the soup.

'Not bad,' he said licking his lips, 'but I think we need a little salt. I don't suppose you have a spot about the house somewhere?'

The old woman got up with surprising agility and soon came back with a bowl of salt.

'Here, soldier,' she said, 'take as much as you need.' The soldier sprinkled some into the saucepan, sat down again and waited. Then, after a few more minutes, he got up and again dipped the spoon into the water and tasted it.

'It's a lot better now,' he said thoughtfully, 'but I

139

think I could improve it if I only had a spot of cabbage to add to it.'

The old woman jumped up and almost ran out, soon to return with a nice healthy-looking cabbage. The soldier placed the cabbage in the saucepan, sat down and waited. A few minutes later he dipped his spoon into the soup and tasted it.

'Fine,' he said, 'but a few potatoes would make it even tastier.'

The old woman lost no time getting an armful of potatoes which the soldier peeled and threw into the saucepan.

This went on until the soldier, by the same means, had also put butter and pepper into the soup. Then he tried it again.

'What's it like now?' asked the old woman.

'Well, it's really wonderfully tasty,' replied the soldier. 'A pity we haven't a bit of meat. That would really give it that extra bit of flavour.' The old woman ran to her larder and returned with a hunk of good red meat which the soldier placed in the saucepan.

'We shall soon have a soup fit for a king,' he said, rubbing his hands and sniffing the appetizing fumes that rose from the boiling water. 'Let's just wait a wee while longer for my axe-juice to really work.'

Finally the soldier decided the soup was ready. The old woman fetched two large soup-bowls and poured out a handsome portion into each one.

The old woman was so delighted with the taste that she brought out a loaf of bread and also a bottle of red wine. They both really enjoyed themselves.

'When do you think the axe will be ready for us to eat?' the old woman suddenly inquired.

'Well, I don't really think it's tender enough yet,' replied the soldier thoughtfully. 'And as I'm in a hurry to get back home to my old mother, I think I'd better take it along with me, as we'll be needing it at home.'

The old woman gave him a very shrewd look but

141

said nothing. Perhaps she understood what he had been up to. Who knows?

Anyway, the soldier got up, thanked her heartily and went on his way.